MALICIOUS

BY
KEVSER AYCAN AŞKIM SAROĞLU

Translated by

Filiz Çiçek

Cover image by

Gülden Bulut

Cover design by

Serkan Yolcu & Yusuf Anar

Publisher

Cosmo Publishing

ISBN 978-1-949872-30-9

Thank you My God for not giving up on me...

Thank you my dear mum, my dad and my whole family and my supportive friends!

Special thanks for Gülden Bulut and Serda Kranda Kapucuoğlu...

Kevser Aycan Aşkım Saroğlu was born in İstanbul... She has graduated from American Language and Literature department of İstanbul University... She has received journalism training in the *Hürriyet Foundation*... She has began her journalism career in the same group... She has worked in *National Geographic Traveler* and *Aktüel* magazines under the **Hürriyet** Group and the Sabah Group... She has worked as an editor and columnist in *Akşam* magazine's weekend journal supplements and *Brunch* **magazine...** She has finalized her journalism days in *HaberTürk*... After, she has done freelance journalism and ghost-writing. She has written for magazines such as *Picus*, *Egoistokur*, and *Derki*... Her first book, *Tutkunun Kum Saati*, was published in 2010. Her fantastic novel, *Darendau'nun Şarkısı*, is still being published by the self-publishing website, *publitory*. As of the December of 2014, she has been working as an advisor for Doğan Novus publishing house... She owns a blog called "Sonsuzlukta Bir Mola Yeri", which covers spiritual subjects... She is also a certified yoga teacher, and she continues educating herself further on yoga, astrology, dreams, spirituality, Islamic mysticism, and energy... She defines herself as perpetual student of life...

Evil wears no costume, but if it did,
it would wear the costume of the good.

But how could you live and have no story to tell?
Fyodor Dostoyevski, White Nights

Summer of 1961, Marrakesh

It's an afternoon in Marrakech, which is called "The Red City" in Arabic, and cherished as "God's Country/ Land" by the native people of Berbers. In one of the neighborhoods at the back of the city, at a rather large square, there was a crowd gathering together once again. This was the marketplace. One of the ordinary marketplaces filled to brim with acrobats, musicians, dancers, story tellers, thread salesmen, silver smiths, and street vendors selling Turkish delights, bagels, sherbet, candy and trinkets.

Again at an ordinary time, there was something that was pulling the crowd right towards the center of the square. It was such a fascinating thing that every single person to come join the crowd had their eyes locked on the same particular spot, as if it was drawing them into its own gravitational field.

Everyone was holding their breaths, watching with complete attention as a boy seated at the dead center of the square looked at some strange shapes laid out in front of him and talked. This square was actually the story-tellers' domain, and the afternoon hours were when they would usually be there, however, there had been no space for the storytellers for a while now. For the past year, that square almost entirely belonged to the kid.

The boy had a scar on this neck, pitch-black eyes that almost struck like lightning wherever they were pointed, and the kind of large, aquiline nose, which was carried like a signet by those who held the most power in this world. The crowd appeared to be captivated by this seven year old boy; whereas he had a look of disdain that was exclusive to those who were born to be the

1

center of attention. It was as if his complete stillness and his lack of response to the gasps around him had granted him a leadership title. With the playful rays of the summer sun, the grains of sand he held in his palm glistened and dispersed around like a waterfall made of gold dust. The boy was actually performing geomancy. While his lips moved silently with an air of mystery, the boy was reading the fates of lives, people and nations from the sand. He was talking of what was to come, and what wasn't.

There was also a considerable number of tourists who were also caught in the boy's spell. The constant clicking of their cameras' shutters indicated that they found the sight this boy to be worthy of photographing.

All eyes in the crowd were fixed on one spot, which made for a precious opportunity for pickpockets and beggars. They did their job as the boy told the future.

After the boy, the second most eye-catching person in that crowd was a woman of Slavic beauty. She was around her 30's, had light blonde hair and eyes like two large, ice blue marbles which observed the boy with great attention. She wore a white shirt and a beige skirt, and she had folded her arms over her perky bosom. Her head was tilted to one side in order to hear the young man who was translating the boy's words for her. The 16 or 17 year old man was enthralled by the beauty of the blonde woman, however, in the meantime he was trying to translate the words of the young geomancer boy, even if it was in short sentences.

The beads of sweat on his upper lip made it more obvious that he was struggling. Before long, the woman was approached by a man in his forties, with the same Slavic features of light blonde hair and fair skin as her. He had also taken to watching the little boy with full attention.

After a while, he turned to the woman and spoke in Russian:

"That's the boy I've been telling you about. What do you think, Irina?"

Never taking her eyes off the boy, Irina responded with tone of certainty:

"You were right, Ivan. He is truly remarkable."

Pleased with his discovery, Ivan said:

"I think he may be useful to us."

"And his parents? What about them?" asked Irina.

"His mother died, and his father ran off. He is currently living here with his grandfather; who let us take the boy wherever in return for a rather small amount of money."

"We will call him Dimitri. What's his real name?"

"Cabbar el Badisi."

Irina raised her eyebrows in slight astonishment, stepped in closer to Ivan, and almost whispering, she said:

"Cabbar el Badisi, huh? That is a powerful name. Good job. He may be quite helpful to us. He has an innate talent for seeing the future and even re-directing it. He might be amongst the brightest alumni of the parapsychology institute."

Ivan smiled and nodded in agreement."

"One day, he will mesmerize the whole world with his talent."

Autumn Of 2012, İstanbul, Kılıç Çiçeği Apartment in Nişantaşı

"Name?"

"Berrak Fazıl."

"Age?"

"Thirty-three."

«Occupation?»

"Freelance."

"What kind of freelance?"

"I own a gift shop."

"Educational background?"

"College graduate; I studied business and management."

"Your reference?"

"Muhteşem Demirci."

"His occupation?"

"Doctor."

"Password?"

"Dwarf."

"Type of application: with or without return?"

"Without."

"With or without blood?"

"..."

Muhteşem had mentioned that they might ask strange questions such as these. What was I supposed to say? I wish I had asked him about it beforehand. Although he did avoid going into detail for some reason. I was so eager, so miserable and so desperate that I didn't think to ask him about it any further. After all, I just needed my problem to be solved. No blood! Blood just runs out, it doesn't solve anything. Can blood wash away the pain?

Why is the secretary staring at me so intently? She has huge eyes. They look like navy-blue balls, with large pupils that are ready to absorb whomever she has her gaze fixed on. She could have had an amazing face had it not been for her tiny lips. Gothic eyes for freakish lips. An entirely cinematographic face.

By all means, I did sense that everything would be a little odd, but now all of this seems to be stranger than I thought. How did ever I decide to jump into this so suddenly? Even so, until this moment, nothing had struck me as unusual; it was as if I were doing what needed to be done all this time. I had convinced myself that everything was perfectly normal. But now, an uneasy feeling is creeping around inside my stomach and it's not letting me go. Everything around me almost radiates eeriness. Darkness beyond words. So be it. I am now at the point of no return. Actually, I can still walk out, but no. I'm not going to back out.

"Without blood."

There; it has gone into record. My application has been saved to that computer. A copy of it has been printed out. It has been processed into a computer and the print out has been placed in a folder with a thick, red cover. Done. I am going to see this through. I have taken the first step beyond the point of no return.

I will not be alone with my suffering anymore, and no more drugs nor alcohol. No cutting, no bleeding. No internal bleeding. It will not end this way, Kerem. You cannot just walk away and leave me high and dry. They say no one can get away scot-free forever, and I hope that's true. I'm here to help destiny on its way. I'm in now. I can't back out.

"If you want the tragedy-scale, the price will increase, but it is amongst our options. Your choice."

"Tragedy."

Yes, make it a small tragedy. I love tragedies. That's what I want, a tragedy. Entirely old, archaic and ancient. Back when we did theatre in university, we had staged many tragedy-centered plays. Tragedy tells the stories of the strong; of those who put forth a claim on life. Where there's power, there's tragedy. Tragedy is the inevitable destination for mortals who defy the Gods, and desire to own their powers. Aren't we all mortals? Then I intend to play this game to the end. I want a Medeian tragedy. Medeia is one of the greatest sorcerers of the ancient world. She is the master of poison and medicine making. She is the daughter of Moon Goddess Hecate, niece of Circe, the Goddess of sorcery. She is the leading character of the longest love epic of the ancient world. She captures the symbol of the rulership of the world; the Golden Fleece, tears down the patriarchy, and is known as the "killer of men" for that reason. Yes, something like Medea.

Pure. Deep. Irreversible, like a knife wound. Like a shard of glass to the eye.

"Miss Berrak; Mr. Cabbar will fill you in on the details at your meeting. That will be fifteen thousand dollars, upfront; with a thirty percent discount included due to being referred by Muhteşem Demirci. Please choose a password."

"You would not have done it."

I think that was the name of a book. That makes for a good password; quite fitting with the occasion. Maybe you would have done it too, Kerem- you have done the other things, after all. But what you and the likes of you do is not penalized, because it is in accordance with social status. Your behavior is seen as a normal one that does not harm our society. It may even be regarded as usual, masculine behavior within the community. What you have done to me does not appear as evil. My inability to turn sharp corners on the road of life is not your fault. On the other hand, what I'm doing now would be regarded as a horrifying act if anyone found out about it. Fortunately, no one will know, and neither will you.

"One last thing, Miss Berrak: In case of a last-minute change of mind about the operation, you need to read the italic text at the bottom of this page and make sure you check that box as well, please."

"Alright, will do."

Why is it written in italic? To draw attention, or to discourage people from reading as italic texts are tiring for the eyes? The latter of the two applies to me. Italic texts are challenging for me. It's better if I don't have to deal with this one on top of all the other challenges of life. Besides, the text is so small that it appears as if they were deliberately trying to make it unreadable. It's as if it was written for ants... Unreadable. I just cannot damage my vision any further with this text right now. It says something along the lines of "should a client back out of the agreement" oh, whatever. Change of mind? For what? My mind is not going to change. If I was going to change my mind, I wouldn't have came here to begin with. I'm in it now. No turning back for me.

"I signed it, there you go."

Weird lips is done with paperwork. She actually looks like a passionate person. Her lips are puckered together as if they are cinched from both sides to keep all that passion from spilling out. Her feet are rather small too, and she's wearing ankle-strap heels which make them look more elegant. Outdated, but still attractive. Perhaps she is Cabbar's lover. She is wearing fishnet stockings, after all. Why do men find fishnets so irresistible? Kerem could not resist them, either. When we met, I was wearing my sexy, deep red fishnet stockings. I wonder if they remind men of some sort of web? They all desire to be entrapped in that web in the very same way that they desire to be crushed under stiletto heels. And later, they fight tooth and nail to get away from that web in which they were entangled by their own will.

But some webs can not be untangled, Kerem.

Some webs are forever, once you're entangled in it, you stay there for good. I have you entangled for life.

Her skin-tight skirt is nice too. Just above knee-length. That is the most seductive skirt length according to men. It's designed to make them want to move upwards. It evokes the same kind of urge that you would get when you see a door left slightly ajar. You can easily walk away from a closed door; even if you are curious about what hides behind it, you would probably decide that it's not worth the hassle. A wide-open door would create next to no urge to explore. But a door that's left ajar is just like a skirt with a slit at the thigh; you just can not walk away from it without satisfying your curiosity.

She would be a total slut if it wasn't for that fine-knit, grayish spinster cardigan of hers. And that "little miss, the star of old black-and-white movies" Belgin Doruk watch on her wrist. My parents adored her, so we would always seek out the classic Turkish Cinema channels to watch the "Little Miss." When I think about it, it's quite clear why my mother liked Belgin Doruk so much: It's because my mother is a "Little Miss" too, and they are rather similar in the sense they are both spoiled.

She is trying to seem innocent by wearing that wool cardigan and that watch; as if to say, "I'm just an ordinary secretary." Then why wear those fishnet stockings and those ankle-strap shoes?

Why do I have such an aversion towards this woman? She reminds me of my mother. My mother is just like her in the sense that her voice is so soft her face carries such a gentle smile that you just cannot believe how her words pierce through you like shards of ice, spoken in that kind voice of hers. Because you think that it's unlike her. Her voice actually carries a poison that gives you deep wounds. Bu you don't realize this at the beginning. You stay in a sweet state of delusion as you slowly bleed out. The poison takes its time to work itself into you.

There are so many cabinets and drawers here. Full shelves, countless drawers and cabinets. Freakish lips fits in well within this room; with all these cabinets and whatnot, they all come together to complete this odd picture. All the drawers are neatly labeled. They remind me of high-tech televisions that are mounted on walls. And they are all dated by day, month, and year.

Wow, the 80's are crowded! They are categorized as 'personal', 'political', 'detective', 'sociological', and 'religious.' Does my file get stored under 'personal'? That second section right there. An entire, huge cabinet is reserved solely for 'love and revenge'. All recorded into small discs. When I'm done, my love will turn into a small disc just like everything else in here. I have to be the first one to make a move and shrink it before it kills me.

Here I am. I still can't believe it. Had I been told several years ago that I would be doing something like this, there is no way I would have believed it. I couldn't have imagined that I would ever come to a place like this more precisely, I couldn't have imagined that a place like here and a concept like this could ever exist in our world. But here it is, as real as can be. Turning thirty-three years old makes you realize that very few things in this world are impossible, if that. They say that thirty-three is when the soul reaches full maturity. Fine then, I have decided to send it into the darkness before it matures completely. It might as well exist in hell from now on, since heaven is already lost.

When you're in your twenties, you believe that the world is exactly—and exclusively—as it seems. That everything is what it seems. You believe that everyone is exactly who they say they are, that everyone's mindset is how they claim it to be. The naivety of youth. When I was young, I used to be like that too; naive, innocent, untouched. Although I had been scratched up, wounded, and beaten down; I had still kept my innocence and faith in life. It was exactly as Scott Fitzgerald had said: "Everybody's youth is a dream." And I believed that I would be living a dream.

There was a time when I was cheerful—despite my mother, who could never get enough of criticizing me, staring me down, and disliking me; and my father, whose face I barely even remember. Despite my mother who never forgot that she only married my father because she was pregnant with me, and never forgave that embryo; I could still smile at life.

But now, I'm here. It still baffles me how I ended up here, but I did. Even though I still struggle with believing that such things exist in our world, and my senses are having trouble with accepting that I'm here, I am. Do people always change for the worse? Do urges become different as they age? I want my urges back. But they will not return. However, I will not be a loser. I won't let that happen.

After everything that happened, I could either come here or lose. Lose, and fall. Deal with those "friendly" faces that turn into sneers the moment I turn my back. Lean on them for picking me up from bars, the ground, pools of my vomit—and even thank them for it. I would even say "You're so great, I love you," out of habit.

Listen to those who preach by saying "You're making a fool of yourself; pull yourself together, and their self-satisfactory, razor-sharp words of which they disguise as pain killers. Put up with them feeling better about themselves by using me because those faces and words are the only thing standing between me anomy loneliness. Let them assume the role of the winner. Be their Gregor Samsa. Turn into a bug so they can feel better about themselves. That's how people are; if they are not doing good themselves, they want someone else to be doing bad. Let them play with me like a toy, lay me on my back and tell me tales of the girl in the red riding hood. As my non-forgiving mother would stare me down with her ice-cold eyes, I would get even smaller for a while. But I can't just accept that. I haven't. I won't.

Kerem is the best thing I have ever had in my life... Well, he *was*.

I'm here so it doesn't have to be *was*.

You were so beautiful. I was completely fascinated. Meeting you made me feel as if I had found out a secret about the universe or the number to solve the grandest mystery of life or the prayer of a mysterious, undiscovered nation. You were the sun, and I was a dark shadow... I'm cold without you.

This is where I escape from my destiny. And that piece of paper is my ticket out. I'm here to skip levels in the scale of fate. So I don't become a loser. Kerem was the best thing that had ever been mine. The lover that everyone was jealous of. The one that draws in envious stares, and makes everyone think "I wish he was mine." Exactly the type of man to fall in love with. Sent as a consolation gift for all that I wanted but couldn't have; and all that I had but lost all these years. A date that has been set up by the angels themselves for me to feel special; as if I had never been lost.

11

Lord, I'm suffering.

I couldn't let him go. His absence makes me physically hurt. My insides feel as if they are burning. I feel like there's a large, red-hot iron pressed up on my ribs, moving up and down. I'm being seared. I'm on fire. I can't move; my knees feel like they've been tied up. This is yearning beyond words. I'm in a never-ending state of thirst; watching a cool, blue waterfall running and churning behind a glass that's absolutely unbreakable. I'm writing unseen letters made of butterfly wings, that run straight into fire with translucent ink. This yearning might just kill me. I will not accept this break-up. I will not watch time go by in that desolate house, with only the hands of the clock as company. I'm not the old Berrak anymore. I'm not clear, I'm murky. I was water, and how I am polluted. I was fire, and now I am ashes. I was air, and now I am scarce. I was earth, and now I am parched.

Let's just start this meeting already and get this nerve-racking wait over with.

You know how everything boils down to just one moment? That one moment in your destiny that completely changes your life, as you know it. That one moment that leaves you feeling like you are no longer a part of your old life. And you don't know for sure what's waiting for you in your new life. That one moment takes place in purgatory. In twilight. That one moment which your eyes don't see, and your ears don't hear, and your feet do not step on; but just felt by your heart. It was a moment like that.

I had known from the very first second I laid eyes on him that the moment I was in was anything but ordinary. I had known him the moment I looked into his eyes. I had known that all this time, I kept running into him, that I had been looking for him.

Even in the first moment, I had felt as if he was closer to me than anybody else I know. I had been caught inside a storm that was nothing like the flutters I had felt before. It felt like a burning of some sort, too. That day was when I first began to understood the meaning of "burning up on the inside." Bombs had been blowing up in my heart. Those bombs were so destructive that it felt as if their booming sounds pierced through cities, tearing the universe apart into its tiniest pieces.

Flames were closing up over cities. Howling sounds were coming from all around. Such an acidic heartache. I had been afraid that he would hear the sound. I had felt it like a sudden aching in the lower part of my body.

"He is the one!" I had said. "The one true love of my life!" But another sentence was ringing from deep within me. A sound echoed through my brain and down to my loins, chanting "He is going to destroy you!" I don't know how I knew it, but I just knew that he is the one.

The phrase "destroy you" was echoing in my soul. I wanted to rattle my mind, mess up everything in it and just erase that phrase from my soul. It was like a foreshadow of a self-fulfilling prophecy. I did the only thing I could possibly do to escape that prophecy, which was burying it within the depths of my subconsciousness, so that was what I did. I drowned it there, but I could feel its existence, its breathing, -even though I couldn't hear it.

I wish I had never heard that sound. But once it had been heard, it could not be unheard.

He was handsome. Sexy. Charming. He had everything I had ever been looking for. He was as good-looking as my father and had a vulnerable side just like him. He was also strong and composed like my mother. He had a laugh that was similar to mine so when he laughed, I almost felt like I was seeing my own self laughing. I had fallen for him, and that was all there was to it. But I had not fallen simply for the way he looked: My eyes had grown used to his eyes, and my soul had gotten to know his soul. The very core of my being had gotten acquainted with the core of his being. This was the kind of intimacy that maybe, only a mother could know after birth. What I felt for him was an impossible desire to be unified. One body, one soul, one mind, one heart.

This had never happened to me before. This was the first time that I had been shaken up with such a feeling.

I knew that when his eyes looked into mine, he could see my soul. And in the same way, my eyes could see his soul as well. The core of his being. Even in that first moment, everything was clear as day. He knew of the earthquakes he caused within my body. My existence, my being was in a drunken trance. I wanted to surrender, but I couldn't. I didn't know how to surrender, I had always been on the other side of that deal. And he was not the kind that would surrender himself. He was not the kind that could be taken. He taught me how to fall in love with my executor. And counting foot steps.

I had loved others too, but Kerem was entirely different. This was the kind of love that told me who I was, that described me. My limits, and the lack there of... The kind of love that revealed all my good sides and bad sides. The kind of love that stood as a mirror to those faces of mine which I had not seen yet. There was no way for me to be without him when my entire being gravitated towards him in the way that flowers turn to face the sun. I just could not exist without him. No, I'm never going to give him away to anybody else. He is mine! He can not be anyone else's but mine.

There had been others that had hurt me in the past. But now it was apparent that they hadn't done much harm at all. And to think,

I had felt so hurt back then. Now I see that they hadn't even left so much as a scratch. It had just been my ego that was hurt. Compared to love, what is ego even worth?

Cem had landed a solid blow on my ego.

Looking back to when Cem broke up with me by a single text message; that had been a rough time for me. Who is Cem anyways? He'se miles and miles away from me now. Cem is just a tiny detail inn my life before Kerem. Not even a comma. Nowadays, everything in my life is split in two: before Kerem, and after Kerem. Although I obviously didn't know this back then. I thought Cem was an important point in my life.

I remember just how much Cem had chased after me back in those days. He had gone above and beyond to be with me. Constant phone calls, running into each other in the most unlikely times and places. Not to mention all the flowers he had sent, and all those expensive, thoughtful gifts he had given me. One time, he asked around to find out which cinema I would be going to and when; to show up in the seat next to mine as soon as the movie had begun. He was trying to surprise me in his own way.

He had been sending me amazing text messages. Always on the pursuit. You know how some people swoop in and clean up your mess for you? That's how he was. He would deal with my things for me. He had all his attention directed to me. He had me all tied up with his constant attention. It was definitely not love, but I guess I got used to being loved. That happens sometimes; you know you're not in love, but it's just so easy to be loved.

Finally his relentless attention and insistence had knocked down my guards; I had accepted his love and after a year of being together, I had even gotten used to him. Yes, I wasn't in love, but it wasn't all too bad. The idea of getting married and starting a family was beginning to grow on me. I had the desire to build the family that I never had. At least, I would get to be a mother. I thought that I would love my child even if I wasn't in love with his or her father. In the meantime, I kept reassuring myself, saying I would not be like my own mother, I guess. Being like my own mother was my worst nightmare.

So, I had finally gotten used to him. The days flew by. Our relationship was moving forward. I thought everything was just fine—not that I cared too much if it was fine or not; my soul was indifferent but my body had surrendered to a different kind of attention—and I had accepted that the rest of my life would be like this. But how can a life go on like that? Even if you were fine with everything, would the other person be content? Finally one day, Cem just disappeared. Almost like he vanished into thin air. I realized that he had left within the same day, because he was the one who was supposed take care of business and go to the store for me. Which was why I cared that someone who had been there for me whenever I needed him was suddenly gone. I was shocked. He wouldn't answer any of my calls. Even his closest friends had no idea where he was or why his phone was switched off. It was unbelievable. I was told that he had quit his job. His house was empty. I felt as if I were in a horror movie. Some kind of desolation. I felt abandoned in an odd sort of way. This feeling of abandonment did not hurt my heart; it hurt my ego. How could he have disappeared without leaving any trace at all? Although he was a Pisces, and Pisces hold the ability to disappear into the depths of the sea as they wish.

And then, after two months, I finally heard from him.

One morning I woke up to this text on my phone screen: "Berrak I'm sorry I couldn't get in touch with you until just now.

I had to get away for a while and think about us. It's not working out. You are a very special person who has a lot of expectations; and I'm just not enough for you. You don't love me. You don't even bother to pretend that you love me. I want a woman who loves me back. And I'm just too tired of your mood swings. I'm sorry. Take care. Hope we can be friends some day."

Idiot... "Too tired"... What could you possibly be tired of? Why would I have a friend like you? Would a person who's worthy of friendship disappear like that? What was the matter? Just not enough for me... It took you an entire year to figure it out? Who did you think I was, just some ordinary woman? Just face me like a man and then talk to me about what's wrong. Why run away?

My pride was hurt at its most sensitive spot. My ego was severely injured. I took it quite hard that someone who had chased after me all this time would just disappear and leave me alone like this. For someone who worshipped the ground you stepped on to just leave...

Leaving had always left a bitter taste in my mouth. Because for every person that left, there was another who was left *behind*. And I always seemed to be the one who was left behind.

They were all leaving. My first boyfriend, Murat, had left me to go study in the U.S. He never returned; instead he married an American girl called Katie who was kindergarten teacher, had long hair, a very plain and wide face and obesity in her future. An ordinary woman who offers a simple happiness. And that was it.

I had actually loved Murat, although not as much as I loved Kerem and not in the same way, either. We had been together since middle school. Perhaps what really united us was our broken-up families rather than the love that we had felt for each other. We were two introverted, self-loathing kids. We had found the sense

17

of family in each other. We actually grew up together, and I always thought that we would get married and grow old together. We would move to the U.S. together; he would go first and figure out the housing and the school, and I would settle things and go join him in 2 or 3 months. Thus, I would have gotten away from my mother for good. But everything fell apart all at once. He hadn't even been there for a month when he met Katie. Supposedly, it was love at first sight. But I know he made this choice so he could live in the U.S.A. with more convenience. And that had hurt me the most.

My love was traded over for convenience. He had broken up with me over a long e-mail. Actually, calling it a letter would be more fitting; as he had written it in letter format. It was the least he could do. He had gone in great detail to explain that he loved me, and why it couldn't work out for us.

Long letter or short, it makes no difference. In the end, it didn't change anything. When a break-up is in question it only comes down to two words: It's over.

All those words had to be strung to one another just to make the end less painful; whereas the conclusion was always: It's over.

No matter how much Murat tried to soften the blow, it still crushed me. It was after breaking up with Murat when I first began to consume alcohol regularly. It calmed me down and helped me sleep... Or pass out. Bars, loud music, dancing and alcohol... It was easier when everything was seen beyond a layer of mist. Every day was a good day to die, every moment was a good moment to drink. Alcohol was like the bandage to my wound. However, my grief would not be going away anytime soon. No matter how much bandage was wrapped around it, it still kept bleeding. This was because the source of the wound was actually not Murat; but my father. With every man I lost, I was losing my father all over again.

Why did they all leave? My father, Murat, Cem? And you, Kerem. I hate being abandoned. No one can abandon me any more. Especially you, Kerem... You will never get to leave.

Actually, if Cem hadn't left then maybe Kerem would never be in my life at all. If Cem hadn't left, I wouldn't have met the love of my life and the most painful heartbreak of my life. Was it significant that the love of my life had arrived upon a goodbye?

Did that mean anything?

Maybe it did, I can't be sure... What about my dreams? Did they have any meaning behind them? My dreams, with all those strange symbols in them? In the cosmic enigma of my life, in the universe of infinite possibilities, were Cem and Kerem connected somehow? Did one have to leave so the other could enter? Maybe it was like that. Maybe everything was connected...

After Cem left, I was quite depressed. I knew that people were talking about me behind my back, whispering to each other that I had been abandoned again. In fact, they didn't even bother to whisper; they talked loud and clear to make sure that I heard. And I heard... I heard it all. I didn't understand why they would want to hurt me like that. I guess they have wanted to hurt me all along. I can't say that I never wanted to hurt anyone. There were two people in my life, which I hurt constantly, and one of them was myself. Hurting myself was one of the things I excelled at. And the other person I had been hurting was the one who had sent me here.

Was it my self-ordained and unyielding stance that brought on all this hatred? Or my charm for which I had done nothing to increase or accentuate? I don't know, maybe it was both. It wasn't my fault that all eyes would turn to me wherever I went. I never made any effort to ensure that. I never wanted to outshine anyone, yet that always ended up happening somehow. I didn't exactly want to draw all the evil eyes onto myself, but they would still find me. It didn't matter how ragged my clothes were, or how unkempt and scruffy I looked: whenever I walked into a party, a bar, or joined a group of people, I would always end up being the center of attention. They would say that my body had some kind of magnetism. Perhaps that was the truth. It felt as if I were carrying a magnet on me that attracted the male gaze. I couldn't quite put my finger on it. In my opinion, it was my eyes that drew them in. There was an unblinking flame in them that reached all the way to my heart.

I suppose that charm was something that originated from one's soul. Attraction had a source that went more than skin deep. It was the appeal of the soul that manifested itself. I carried chaos within me, and it was the appeal of chaos that made me so desirable. Wasn't life itself a chaos? Weren't we all looking for the cosmos inside the chaos? And the chaos inside the cosmos? Apparently, the red flame of the volcano inside me could be seen from the outside. My soul, which had been searching for a peaceful harbor; was being rattled by the never-ending earthquakes inside the chaos.

What they didn't understand was that attractiveness cannot be obtained with make up, clothes, or such other things. Beauty comes from the soul. It was the light radiating from the struggle of my soul trying to free itself from the chaos within that made me shine and set me apart from others. I had something completely fatal, yet completely alive.

According to my mother's constant jabs and insinuations made in the most inappropriate times—and repeated constantly, often at the cost of humiliating me—I had inherited my love for alcohol from my father. I have no idea how so many of his organs could fail simultaneously at such a young age, but he was just forty-two years old when he died. It must have been how he wanted to have his final round with my mother. He took his revenge by dying. Since he was a Pisces, he made his impact silently. Slyly, even. His death was befitting to a Pisces. He turned into a fish in the Rakı bottle. He drowned at the drinking table, accompanied by bottles and bottles of booze. My mother is a beautiful, cold, and rare woman. My father was a handsome, sweet, and weak man. Yet they were in love. They had attracted each other. Theirs was love, too. But as a Capricorn woman, my mother had enough of this weak Pisces man over time. Never ending fights in the house, followed by long periods of icy silence. And my infinite loneliness. My father was a graphic designer with the soul of a poet, and my mother was an insurance agent without a hint of poetry in her soul. In the Zodiac, it is said that Capricorn's tail is Pisces. So those two signs—one being incredibly emotional and the other being completely realistic—are like each other's shadow. Clearly my mother was looking for an antidote to her coldness in my father, and my father was looking for a body that could withstand his own weakness in my mother. But it did not work out. After a while, my mother had gotten sick of my father's weakness and drinking. In her eyes, he was now a loser who had lost all his appeal; someone who's not worth securing. On the other hand, my father wanted a mother to whom he could bare his soul. However, every day he came home to an ice-cold woman. He wanted to be accepted as he was. Unconditionally. And my mother just couldn't accept a man like that. And then there were other women, infidelity, leaving the house, plenty of alcohol –drugs, even– and finally, death.

And a lonely child.

That was me...

My mother hadn't even noticed me until my father's death. I was a child with a mother who performed her maternal duties but did not love her child; and a father who loved his child but barely even saw her.

I was alone, and I grew up with the pain of solitude.

My father's death didn't affect my family's financial situation. And for my mother, he had stopped existing a long time ago anyways. Maybe he never did. In terms of money, my father had joined the Kerim family feeling lowly. And he stayed that way. Nihat Fazıl had never really been a Kerim, and Zuhal Kerim had never really been a Fazıl. We had inherited my grandmother's 3-story mansion at the Island; which had been bought by selling the land that belonged to my grandmother's former Ottoman admiral father.

Plus we had the money that my mother was making in the insurance business. We were never short of money, but we were short of love. Actually that wouldn't exactly be true, because how can you be short of something that you never had in the first place? Love was something that I never really knew, but always longed for. And since I'd never been given love, I didn't know how to give it to somebody else either. But I was Nihat Fazıl's daughter after all, so my heart craved love. I was looking for it in other people. People who didn't have any love to give to me. In men who looked like my father and acted like my mother. In men with ice-cold hearts. In handsome, weak men.

I hit rock bottom after Cem left. I hit rock bottom as if I had fallen inside a well. The wounds from losing my father bled again. The wounds from losing Murat bled again. So I wanted to wash away the blood with alcohol as a habit I had learnt from my father. A habit was the only thing that made me feel any closer to my parents, so I chose my father.

In those days, I had begun drinking almost every day. My insatiable thirst was not for alcohol, but for forgetting. I was thirsty to forget. To forget and become numb. That was all that I wanted. I was making a harsh u-turn.

Some days I would drink at home. I would drink one Brandy coffee after the other. I liked it. It was good and stiff. Not to mention safe for social situations, too. It looked like I was drinking a cup of coffee, and it did a great job at getting me drunk. At that period, drinking at home was better than drinking at bars. This was partially because the was no one there to try and pull me on my feet. I could just drink, pass out, forget everything. An eternal escape was calling out to me, and I had no intention of turning back.

I had begun staying home all the time. I wasn't even going to the store anymore. I was on a downward spiral.

My store was actually nice. It was my own personal shrine. As I graduated from business school, my mother realized that I could never hold a corporate job—or any kind of job for that matter—so she put in the funds to create my shrine. It was true a nine-to-six job wasn't for me, and neither were complying with orders I didn't agree with, putting in my time for a job I didn't believe in, nor trying to have some kind of life by meeting with my friends at those limited and precious couple of hours after work. I could not live part-time. My soul, which alternated between a full-time life or no life at all; refused to be a slave. I was already a slave to my own suffering. The last thing I needed was having a boss like my mother. And she made the shop for me because she knew this. I suppose it was her last-ditch effort to keep me alive. Her maternal responsibilities must have outweighed her heart of store.

It was a gift shop which offered clothes, miscellaneous souvenir items, small alarm clocks, jewelry, pencils, mirrors, accessories, weird rings, dangly earrings, tiny purses, decorations, trinkets, hearts, cat-shaped pillows, bells, gloves, masks, tea cups, candles, incenses, life-like plastic flowers, clocks that don't show the time, photo frames of every size, hand-held fans, bobbing-head dog figures, curled up plush cats, fuzzy socks, belts, and any other knick-knacks that you can think of. It looked like a total deray. On the first couple of days after the shop had opened; I gathered up some vitality, and personally picked and bought every single item that I would be selling at the shop. I had taken care of my shrine.

Inspired by the Bülent Ortaçgil song, I named the store "Şık Latife."(Fancy Latife [Jest]) In reality, there was nothing fancy nor jestful about the situation. The shop was completed by a young woman in unkempt clothes who drank Brandy and smoked cigarettes amidst all those knick-knacks. Every once in a while, I would take the time to dress nicely. On those days, I would be the most interesting piece in the shop. Truth be told, my shop wasn't exactly a wonderland. Yet almost every day, one or two people would come in, take a close and careful look at some items, pick them up to inspect them further, and most of the time leave without buying anything. I was just like those items in my shop: Everybody looked at me, but nobody took me in. Nobody claimed me as theirs and put me on their nightstand. So I could never figure out where exactly I belonged in this world. I could not put down my roots and I could not belong.

As a matter of fact, I didn't even care about my shrine anymore. As of late, I didn't even drop by. My shrine was as good as abandoned. I didn't have it in me to go to Mahmutpaşa, Tahtakale, or Kapalıçarşı to stock up on items for the shop. I just didn't feel like it. I just drank in the embrace of my depression. I hired a young girl to sit at the counter.

While I did appreciate her dedicated efforts to make sales, I was unwilling to do so much as lift a finger for anything. My soul was tired and I felt as if it would stay tired forever.

Answering the phone felt like too much work. I didn't want to communicate with anyone. So for most of the time I was out-of-order.

However, everything has a turning point. Sometimes your destiny is changed by the decision to answer a call or not. Sometimes everything is determined by picking up, or not picking up. Sometimes destiny weaves its web through phone lines. Which happens to be a rather useful way to weave webs in the twenty-first century. I love how destiny updates itself to keep up with the changing times. The courtroom called destiny uses whichever technology is the newest, or shall I say; the hook of karma digs deep...

On one of those days, my phone started ringing. And it rang on and on so insistently that I just picked it up. I don't know if it happens to anyone else, but sometimes I feel like the same old ringtone rings with a different kind of urgency. I know you would think it's just selective perception, but it's not that. The energy, the urgency, and the motive of the caller as they make the call changes the usual rhythm of the ringtone. Sometimes there is such a heavy-charged energy on the other side of the phone that you just can't resist. That was exactly what happened to me.

The beginning of everything was the moment I answered that call.

It was Timur.

My old friend Timur had accompanied me through the twists

and turns of my fate. He's an interesting man with a wide social circle. As he knows exactly how to rise up on the stairs of life; he hangs out with rich and successful people and surrounds himself with such people. That's how he has managed to make money with no money at all to begin with. His fund is his mind, and keeping close to strong people. He's in the right place at the right time. He knows when to leave the ship as well as he knows when to board it. Well, he is right in his own way; he wanted to rise, so he did. And in this part of the world, the way to achieve this is not working very hard; it's knowing the right people. On the other hand he's funny, nice and he likes me. We are childhood friends as we grew up in the same neighborhood. He's older than me by a year or two. And I managed to earn his affection somehow, even though I didn't do anything to earn it. It's strange how sometimes you put your whole life on the line and win nothing; and sometimes you win even though you really haven't done much at all... Well, I had Timur without any real effort whatsoever. After the usual greetings were exchanged, Timur cut right to the chase.

"Berrak, you've been depressed for more than long enough. You're coming over to my place tomorrow evening. I'm throwing huge party."

"Timur, I can't even get out of the bed, let alone go partying."

"You have until tomorrow to get yourself out of the bed, and that's that."

"Timur, I haven't even brushed my hair for days. Forget it. Do you really think I can make it to a party?"

"Are you really going to hurt my feelings like that? Just come over. You're beautiful no matter what, even if your hair is filthy. Just come."

"I can't..."

"Yes, you can. Come over and hang out for a couple of hours. I just got some great whiskey. The music's good. Come, drink, be merry! What's the worst thing that could come out of it? And I missed you. Get out of your cave already! Come on, I'm not taking no for an answer. And if you don't come, I'll come over there and drag you out by force."

Timur was relentless. He was so insistent that I had to tell him I'd be there just to get him off my back. However, I wasn't actually planning to go anywhere, and I most certainly didn't want to leave the house. I was hell-bent on staying home.

As it turns out, I would be going to the party after all. I would be at the party, and from that moment on my life would change. Turns out my destiny has been invited to the party as well, and I would be going towards it. Turns out that destiny's latest trick would be disguised as a party this time.

You know when things start to pick up their speed, everything just pushes you towards the fastest direction? Well, the minute I got off the phone with Timur, my doorbell rang. It was my "best friend" Yıldız, who I hadn't seen for a long time. Yıldız and I had grown up together, and just like Murat, she had also witnessed my difficult childhood. We went to primary school, middle school, high school and university together. Yıldız was like my opposite. She was as tidy as I was messy; as sane as I was crazy; as sensible as I was crazy in love. As in control of herself as I was a mess. As engaged as I was abandoned.

As Yıldız hadn't been blessed with any trace of empathy nor the ability to sense what goes on around her; she would pay no mind to my mental breakdown, nor bother with being kind when she spoke. According to her, the truth was the truth and there was nothing wrong about stating it in any occasion. She started speaking by pointing her words, which were filled with poisoned arrows, straight to my heart.

"Berrak, look at yourself! It's the same thing all over again. See, you're thirty years old now and dumped again! You're back to your dark, depressed nights and drinking alone. You are destroying yourself. It's the same thing once again. Just when you reach the stage when marriage is in question, the men suddenly say "Bye!" What do you do to these guys? They all run without looking back and then marry somebody else... Just go to Timur's party. Stop stalling. You're only hurting yourself, not anybody else. Go and prove to yourself that life goes on!" She just snapped at me with all this. Did you choose the word *bye* on purpose, Yıldız? Just *bye*. Not even *goodbye*. So insignificant and brief. Such an insincere word for parting ways. Such a cheap way to break it off. Well, this is just how Yıldız is: whether it's on purpose or not, she can manage to hurt people profoundly.

I was hurting myself, indeed. In my opinion, one always had the right to devastate and destroy oneself. And I was exercising that right of mine to its full extent. Yet deep inside I knew Yıldız had a point. Unfortunately that didn't make me want to punch her on the nose any less. I had such anger towards her that had been accumulating all these years, and she just acted like she had no idea how I felt. It was more convenient for her, as her most basic strategy was pretending she had no idea. I knew she was actually right. I hated that she was right and I hated how she could just say it to my face so bluntly. That was just how Yıldız was.

She was right, because a short while after our break up, Cem had gotten engaged with one of his old friends from school. Yıldız loves to do this; in fact she makes it her duty to tell me all this, to pretend to be a real friend as an excuse to keep hurting me. It makes her feel so high and mighty. Verbal masturbation. Orgasm for know it alls. Since I dare to go right to the heart of life, she retaliates every time I fall. I know this, yet I still let her do it. She's temperate and steady she always knows what to do and exactly how she's going to do it. She has an unfaltering sense of moderation. She never drinks more than two glasses of alcohol, never gains weight, never wears ragged clothes, never raises her voice. She doesn't even cry. She has managed to be in a relationship with the same guy for twelve years and lived a completely risk-free life. So she can give good advice. She doesn't hesitate to make judgements about things that would never happen to her. Everybody has a friend like this, and mine happens to be Yıldız. In spite of it all, I still love her: She's reliable and she never goes behind my back. Feeling better about herself by making me feel worse in such situations is her only flaw. She pulls me towards risks that she hasn't experienced. She's my other half; the stable person that I wish to be from time to time.

Yıldız kept harping on about how I could meet some new people at Timur's party. In fact, she was sure that I would come across somebody new to love, which she kept implying repeatedly. Actually, she wasn't implying. She had said it loud and clear: "You'll definitely meet someone new." With that know it all attitude. "One nail drives out the other," was her closing line, even though she had only driven one nail in her entire lifetime. Which she didn't even have to to drive out. I, on the other hand, didn't care about nails or anything. I didn't want new love. I actually didn't want anything at all. I just wanted to drink a bit, take my mind off things and just forget. I was the daughter of an alcoholic father. Genetics did exist, after all. What I wanted was to be numb all the time. But as Yıldız would say, I was going to go looking for nails.

And then Yıldız, who had a steady relationship with a guy who adored her for twelve years, and then married him when it was the right time to do so, comes over and asks me "What do you do to these guys?" in her usual, high-and-mighty way.

There's the deadly question...

What do I do these guys? I don't know. I want to love passionately. I want a man's soul. I want us to become one completely; in soul, body, and mind. I want him to belong to me and I want to belong to him. I want to have what that really old Turkish classical music song describes. Whenever I hear this song in those black-and white Turkish movies that I watch with my grandmother, I feel like it describes me. As Türkan Şoray runs around meadows and hills to find Ediz Hun; Zeki Müren sings in the background with his pure and profound voice: "Desire on your lips/The only one in your arms/ The only one who's in love with you/ Let me be only one, darling... Accompanying your days and nights/ The only one as the teardrop in your eye/ The only one who's in love with you/ Let me be the only one, darling..."

Yes this is what I want. Something like what the song mentions. I want their souls. I do it.... So they go to somebody else...

Yıldız kept being pushy, and then Timur called again. I don't know if it was because destiny was too determined to weave its web; because I wanted to get rid of Yıldız and Timur's relentless nagging; because I wanted to spite them; or because subconsciously I wanted to get out of this situation too; but I finally decided to go to the party. And the process which led me here began on that day, when I went to that party. Everything is so connected to each other! There really are no gaps.

It's been twenty minutes, and I just want it to be my turn so I can go and talk to this guy. Waiting, waiting, and then some more waiting. I'm bored and fed up. Come on already, I can't take this for much longer. Why are they making me wait so much? I did get an appointment beforehand to arrange this meeting. I have an appointment. And it was arranged by Muhteşem himself! They cannot offend Muhteşem. Why are they making me wait so much? I just want to go inside and get this over with already...

Every moment, every detail of the day and night of the party is still so vivid in my mind, I still remember everything about that twist of fate... About all those things that happened to me.

The meeting of two personalities is like the contact of two chemical subsances: if there is any reaction both are transformed.

Carl Gustav Jung

Summer of 2009,
terrace floor of the lotus apartment in Cihangir,
three years ago

The party had continued into the night. These were the hours when everybody was "hammered", and the booze and the smoke made it much easier to be intimate. Timur's terrace looked out to the Bosphorus scenery in all its glory. The night lights of İstanbul, with their reflections on the sea, had made the atmosphere more mysterious, more inviting and more open to pleasures. It was as if the lights bouncing off the Bosphorus waters had transformed the entire city into an exceptional, twilight nightclub of wild pleasures, in which everything was possible. And it felt like this place was the center of it all. In every corner of Timur's house's spacious living room, shadows in close embraces had already begun their intimacy sessions. All the love hormones fluttering around had filled the atmosphere with the energy of the night, and for some, the smell of one night stands were in the air. In the night, souls were as far away from each other as two separate universes; yet bodies seemed to get drawn closer and closer to each other inside one world. And I was sitting in a corner, drinking by myself.

I had finally decided to show up. And once that decision was made, I was taken over by a strange energy. I had gotten out of bed, showered, applied some hair care products to my hair, and I had even gone out to get a mani-pedi. Deep burgundy polished nails, deep burgundy painted lips. If I were a color, I would be deep burgundy. Mysterious, uncanny, attractive, spiritual…

I had also taken some time to decide what I would wear. Since

I would be going there to 'drive out a nail', I might as well wear something that serves as a tight pair of pliers. I had to be seductive, I had to be a wine-toned burgundy, I had to look naughty enough, bold enough, tempting enough. I had to cover up all the hurt I carried inside me with all those sexy clothes I owned. That was what clothes were good for, anyways… My skin-tight black mini skirt; fishnet stockings; burgundy top that falls off on one shoulder; and my stilettos… My deep burgundy lipstick, smoky eyes. When I stepped in front of the mirror to take a look, the woman in front of me appeared to be promising enough. After all, if you manage to be promising, the rest will follow. It was like all the success of capitalism. It doesn't matter if it can be done or not, just make promises… Just have hope.

My mother had watched this long preparation process through squinted eyes. I couldn't tell if there was concern or a hope for salvation behind them. I was finally dressed up and going out, this was a big deal… I guess she was trying to understand what I was trying to do. Well, she couldn't understand, because neither could I.

The night had blended all the shadows into one another, but this party was slowly starting to turn into a nightmare for me. There were a few sets of eyes following me, but fortunately no one dared to approach me, as I was clearly unwilling to communicate. All these crème de la crème people were simply repulsive to me. Journalists, advertisers, PR agents, businessmen and businesswomen, writers, curators… I had no business in an arena in which everyone was trying to display themselves. I was cursing myself for coming here despite knowing all this. This fake-paradise party was really starting to bum me out. Timur came over a couple of times to make small talk and try to introduce me to some people against my will; but my silence kept any of the conversations from moving any further. I didn't like any of the people I met. The nail I had been looking for was not here. They all seemed like pretentious, soulless bodies to me.

I wasn't actually looking for a nail; but for some reason, I felt as if something interesting would happen at this party, and so did everyone else. I was at ease when I drove everyone away from me with my ice-cold energy. They could look if they absolutely had to, but they could not get too close. And the rest was easy.

The party was crowded, the music was loud, the view was beautiful, and the booze was plenty. Wasn't drinking and hanging out what I wanted to do anyways? I sprawled out over a soft cushion with my fishnet-clad feet pointing to the nightclub view of the Bosphorus. And I had brought along a bottle of Jack Daniels as company. I had simply smiled in response to the surprised looks of the waiter who tried to hand me a glass as I refused and only took the bottle. As far as I was concerned, everything was going well for now.

The setting was just right for getting lost in thoughts and for immersing myself fully into my pain and sorrow. It attracted me, as did every other setting that was close to rock bottom. So I was doing just fine… But then…

Have you ever felt like a moment was approaching; like you were about to step into a life-changing moment any second? Would you be able to feel it? Would the energy precede the moment? I think it would. And it did. All of a sudden, I felt an odd warmth spreading inside me. My heart was tingling even though there was nothing going on. Turns out, there was…

As my cigarette smoke rose to the sky in ringlets and a light breeze caressed its way through my hair, I was suddenly startled by a hand over my breasts.

Just as I jumped up with fury, I saw a pair of dark eyes. They were as shiny as a pair of glossed leather boots. When I looked at him, I felt a strange chilling sensation crawling up my spine, and at once, the strange dream I had the other night flooded into my memory.

A strange dream had interrupted my sleep the other night. I dreamt that there was a young man in a smoke-grey suit next to me. I was wearing a half-green, half-red, flowy dress and I was barefoot. I was walking hand in hand with this man whose face I could not see. I was trying, but no matter how much I turned my head to take a look, I could not see his face. We kept walking towards the rocks that were ahead. There was a strong wind blowing my hair all around, and it almost swept me off my feet. As we were moving towards the rocks, the sea was beating them with furious waves. The wind picked up its speed and finally got so rough that it ripped the green piece off of my dress. I was left with only the red part of my dress. Then, a hill appeared before us. Perched on it was a gold colored bird that looked like an eagle. There was a cat next to the bird. And then, a violent sandstorm began; and right then, the man whose hand I had been holding just disappeared. Upon his disappearance, a hand like an iron claw grabbed my heart with a grip that got increasingly tighter. It was like an iron hand from the Middle Ages. Just then, I saw an enormous eye, which started to suck me inside, and I disappeared inside the eye. I remember waking up drenched in sweat. I had been scared, spooked, but unable make sense of the dream. But I had always had movie-like dreams such as this. I didn't really dwell on why I had them, and didn't spend any more time thinking about them. So why was I remembering that dream now, and upon looking at this man? What was he trying to tell me?

He had gently placed his hand on the silver chain around my neck that reached down to the end of my cleavage. He was playing with my necklace, which was made of moonstone and had 'Scorpio' written on it. His beautiful hands brushed the area where my breasts were. It wasn't my breasts that he touched; it was my heart. My heart, which was suffering now.

He was one of those guys who knew how to seduce someone with small gestures. The kind of man whom you cannot be mad at for too long. The kind who is sexy even when he's violent; in fact, the kind who makes you want him to attack.

He said, "Scorpio, huh? So you're a Scorpio. Scorpio women are within my field of interest." His hands remained on my necklace…

I had found it hard to believe that the man standing before me was real. You know the saying 'too good to be true'? That was spot on in that situation. He was too enchanting to love me. Too convincing for me to believe him. Too magnificent to be mine. Could it be? Was he real? I looked directly in his eyes and asked, "What do you know about Scorpios?"

With his voice that had the sexiness/sexy tone that came from being a long time smoker, he said, "Well, I know that they know how attractive they look in burgundy fishnet stockings, a black velvet mini skirt; and a burgundy top that falls off on one side to reveal their gorgeous, glowing shoulder."

So he had seen me. So he had been aware of me for a long time. So I had entered his world without noticing it myself. Otherwise how could he have described my clothes down to every detail, at once? It had made me feel amazing that he had paid so much attention to my clothes. So he had been observing me from head-to-toe for a while now. So, how come I hadn't seen him? He must have had arrived later. The man standing in front of me was a total nail; a concrete nail, at that. This must have been what Yıldız had been talking about. And now, this man was inviting me to a game, to a circus of wonders… I had suddenly risen out of my depression like a phoenix rises from its ashes, and I had decided to jump into the mysterious and irreversible playing field of love with my entire being. I suppose that was the moment I had been waiting for my entire life. I was walking towards the full moon of true love.

If he wanted to play, then I was going to play along.

"Don't be fooled by Scorpio women's appearance," I blurted out.

He said, "I know Scorpio is the sign of sex, darkness, and the underground." His smile descended down my throat like a cup of chocolate. My eyes caught a curve that appeared on the side of his mouth as he smiled, and I wanted to touch it with my tongue. I wanted to devour that curve entirely. To have it inside me. Of course I held back, but I guess he had been able to sense this desire, this energy, from my eyes.

He had a smile that was hard to resist. The dimple on his chin gave him an elusive yet childish appearance. It made me want to throw myself a him and take him in my arms at the same time. What a strange feeling… And I had loved it. I had never felt like this before. Apparently, I had arrived at some unknown terrain within my own existence. No one had ever stepped into this pristine place inside the geography of my soul. It was like a desert's awakening. It was a morning beyond words.

I was under a spell. I felt like the ground beneath my feet was slipping. Just as Atilla İlhan had written, I had earthquakes inside me, and the fear of suicide. Was it possible for one person to evoke so many different emotions in me at once? Much like dogs that could smell fear, my subconscious was warning me about the dangers of this man I was facing. It kept saying, "This man can destroy you," over and over again. It was as if this signal had been adhered to my brain with some invisible glue. "He can tear you apart, he's nothing like Murat or Cem, this man will break you like your father did…" Humans' urge to get rid of the thing they love out of fear is strong. I loved this self-fulfilling prophecy and I wanted to get rid of it. Something like that old saying: sometimes you kill the one you love the most.

I felt an irresistible urge to break that moment, to break everything. I was being rattled by such a strong energy that I got scared of the explosions it caused inside me, and I panicked. I was afraid that this energy would swallow me whole and take over my existence. I wanted nothing to start. Ruin the game before it begins. I had sensed the danger.

I said, "Then you must know that Scorpios sting." In the meantime, I was smiling without ever moving my eyes away from his. I don't know why I was smiling. I guess a war was being fought in my heart, my brain and my body between the impulse to run for my life and the impulse to stay and get attached. How strange; when I first saw him, I immediately felt that I wanted him to love me and to stay by his side forever. What a moment it was; at once I wanted a total stranger to be mine forever and run away from him without leaving a trace. Fear and love were pushing down on my heart, side by side. But which one would win? Which one was I rooting for?

With his fatal smile, he continued, "I sense a threat. Danger moves me. Its impact on me is like that of a hot spice. I like spicy. Danger befits a woman; it adorns her. As a matter of fact, hatred is erotic, too."

I slowly moved my fishnet-clad, shapely legs to the side and made room for him to nestle up to me. I knew the basic moves I had to make by instinct: I was a Scorpio woman after all.

It was attraction that began in the very first moment. Love at first sight. We were both aware that our encounter was an extraordinary one.

We began to talk as our breaths caressed one another. I found out that his name was Kerem. He was a publisher. He owned Çilek (Strawberry) Publishing House, which published top-selling literature and self help books, grew more and more everyday, and became one of the leading publishing houses in the sector. "Why is it called Çilek?" I asked him. Turns out the name was a reference to Nastassja Kinski, who was a famous actress back in the day. He told me the story. Even though it was a story, I was jealous. Jealousy. That poison had entered my system the moment I saw him. I wanted to keep this man—whom I knew nothing about except that I wanted him to be mine forever—away from every single woman on the face of the earth. Including those from his past. Here was the first sign from the very beginning. The danger kept growing. This love was going to drive me insane. When he was thirteen years old, Kerem "came across" a movie called Tess starring Nastassja Kinski "by coincidence", and he watched it. Back when the movie was made, Nastassja Kinski was very beautiful. Even though she was well over mid-age now and there was no trace of her beauty left, apparently she was gorgeous back then. In this movie, there was an erotic scene where Nastassja Kinski swallows up a huge strawberry with her full, red lips. As a 13 year old, he was so impressed by this scene that from that point, Nastassja became his childhood crush. He kept repeating that scene in his mind. Strawberries were his favorite fruit since then.

He also believed that strawberries brought him luck. Strawberries, which had been imprinted into the memories of his childhood, ended up naming the publishing house he had dreamt of having. Strawberries have been lucky for him...

"Whenever I'm upset, I just picture Natasha in that scene. It entertains me," he said, as he looked into my eyes and smiled. I couldn't even let the daydream of a woman whose days of beauty were left in the past to have him. We got closer to each other, like animals that approached each other for mating without a hint of hesitation in their steps. It was as if we were in a magnetic field, the attraction was so strong that we couldn't stop it even if we wanted to. Our breaths were touching. Our eyes were locked to one another's. He traced my lips with his index finger. Then he grabbed my hair and pulled me close to himself. He held me tight. I was completely enfolded in his embrace; which was where I wanted to be for the rest of my life. Our lips became interlocked. I felt his tongue on mine. After that moment, we were inseparable.

We were aware of the wild attraction between us. After kissing, I guess he got scared of his feelings like I did, and wanted to put a stimulant, some kind of distance between us. A destructive bomb brought on by fear. With a few buzzkill words, he wanted to create a distance between us that never existed in the first place. I had sensed that he was scared I would take hold of him. He had a point. That was exactly what I intended to do. To corner him. I could see the depth of his fear. I was a Scorpio, and Scorpios could sense the deepest fears of people.

He was humming, "Let's drink tequila. I like women, speed, and tequila. 'Welcome to Tijuana, tequila sexo marihuana...'" It was a song from Latino musician Manu Chao.

I paid no mind. Instead, I decided to call his bluff. I was not going to fall for it.

I said, "I love Manu Chao, especially that song. I see you know quite a bit about the astrology."

With his irresistible smile, he said, "Astrology is an effective method for picking up girls. I have to know a thing or two about it. After all, I publish self-help books, too. Astrology books sell well these days." Then he brought his face closer to mine, and said, "Women want to be figured out." That made me incredibly angry. He couldn't just generalize me along with the rest of the women in the world. Generalizations might be useful in explaining social issues, but they are usually deadly in intimate relationships. I wanted to be special; I couldn't be squeezed into generalizations. I did not like his stereotypical, manly actions and his cliche flirting style. It was strange that I didn't expect such cliches from him; I didn't even know him.

What he did was a typical man trick; a dirty one at that. Supposedly he was just playing the game, but why did he have to interrupt our amazing tango with this cheap music? Then he backed away slightly. He smiled and continued: "Plus, I like my sign. I have all its characteristics. Pioneering, bold, adventurous, sexy..."

I said, "Aries!" and added, "Can't be tied down easily."

"Depends on how you tie them up," he said as he laughed and pushed back a lock of hair that had fallen over my forehead. He got closer and whispered in my ear. His bottom lip was at the tip of my earlobe and our breaths were entangled. I felt his teeth reach my earlobe and bite down very gently. Suddenly, I felt millions of tiny flames light up inside me, all at once as if someone flipped a switch.

There was wind and I was on fire.

He continued. "You look like someone who knows how to tie somebody up. May I learn the name of my Mistress?"

I answered, "Berrak." I was expecting the usual storm that my name always caused, but he looked into my eyes with disbelief and burst out laughing.

He said, "Who would think of naming such an assertive, sexy and mysterious Scorpio woman 'Berrak'?" He continued with a teasing smile: "There is no way you can be 'Berrak'; you are dark, private, mysterious, complex…" Then he pretended to put on a serious face and said, "I sense something precarious about you, I better not make you angry." Seeing as I'm here now, it's safe to say to he was right. It's best not to make me angry.

He could feel me. He could see into my depths. Maybe I did have something precarious about me. It was dangerous for me that he would describe me like that; that he could reach so deep into me. That he knew all about my darkest zones, all of my weaknesses… The danger bells rang loud and clear; if I didn't spoil the game right now and allow him into my life, I could sense that I would be miserable again.

The universe sent one warning signal after another. I would be broken beyond repair. I was scared. My deepest fear was stirring. If I were to fall out of this love, I would not survive. So I decided to spoil the game even further, to emasculate him.

"My mother thought of it," I hissed. "And my father went along with it, he didn't have any other suggestions. Maybe he would, had I been a bottle of liquor… My mother wanted to have a clean, pure, proper daughter. Unfortunately for her, she didn't get what she wanted. I'm nothing like what my mother wanted me to be; I've never been, and I'm quite glad that I'm not. If you knew my mother, you would agree with me. Trust me," I told him.

45

I had spoiled the mood enough and turned it ice cold; and along with it I had also ruined the afterglow of the party, as well both our moods. I was spiteful and gloomy. Yet I was still in his arms. I thought he would leave me and go away, thus ending the danger, but…

"Ooh, a sad story. Your voice got higher and higher as you spoke. You started to talk through your teeth, as if you were hissing. Are we at the edge of danger? Do I sense that you have a mild hatred towards your parents, or am I mistaken? It's as if aggressive words have been spilling through these beautiful lips. That's fine, the absence of a father makes a woman eerily attractive. Did they not spoil you enough, little girl? But as I told you before, I like danger. And I like spoiling…"

Wrong life cannot be lived rightly

Theodor Adorno

Autumn of 2012, İstanbul, Kılıççiçeği Apartment in Nişantaşı

"Miss Berrak, Mister Cabbar is expecting you, you may go inside."

Yes, it's finally time. Now I'm going past the point of no return. I have been finding consolation by laying in my bed and thinking of this moment for a long time, and yes, I am ready now. Yes, I am anxious, but I don't know if it's more about the possibility of nothing happening rather than what's going to happen. If this doesn't work, I don't have a plan B. I don't have a future to look forward to. My future is gone with Kerem. Buried under the sea. Anyway, it's no good to think about these things now. Right now, I have to focus on Cabbar el Badisi. Since I am crossing a threshold, I might as well do it properly and with no return.

Oh my God, so this is Mister Cabbar's room!

Incredible. So, where is he? I was told he was been waiting for me, but he isn't here yet. What a strange office! So large, and so many edges. It has a strange shape, almost like a hexagon. Is it possible for a room to be hexagonal? I have never seen it done before. The walls are orange, and the carpets are mainly red. The flowerpots by the window are so huge. And they all have the same, rubbery plants with large leaves. But I haven't seen these plants before. Why do all the pots have the same plants and why are they lined up side by side? There is also a big, metallic table that has been placed in the center of the room, sprawling out like a gigantic octopus.

One side of the room opens out to a wrap-around terrace.

Through the windows, I can see trees full of green leaves. You would think it was some meditation center to find peace or something. Everything besides the walls and the carpets are all crisp white. What about that enormous white table? Is this a joke? I can't believe this, there are three large screens set inside the table. But there isn't a single cable or any kind of electrical part in sight. Then how do those screens even work? They did a good job hiding the cables. Cutting-edge technology. Right by the terrace, there are two large armchairs covered in white leather. I wonder if that's where we will be sitting.

What is that? What's up with the large notebook on the white, round coffee table between the armchairs? There are patterns on the coffee table. But they are… Interesting patterns… They are all shaped like eyes. How strange, they look like that eye I have seen in a dream. And the wall right across is covered from the ground and all the way up to the ceiling with the giant, green leaves of the potted plants. That part of the room almost looks like a jungle. Oh dear God, there is a metal swastika hanging from the ceiling over the table. What does this mean? Is Cabbar secretly a Hitler fan?

And the calendar on the wall starts on day zero of the month. How can a calendar start on day zero? A timeline that begins with nothing. I guess it's possible; I came here knowing who Mr. Cabbar is, and what he is going to do. There are yin-yang symbols in small, round frames hung on all the walls. Female and male, night and day, light and dark, black within the white, white within the black. Why is this guy so obsessed with yin yangs? I can't make sense of it.

Anyway, I better just get seated on that white armchair. Besides, I think I hear some footsteps outside the door. I think he's coming. God, my heart is pounding so fast that it might just fling itself out of my mouth and through the window, turn into a bird and fly away. My chest feels tight. A part of me wants to get out of here. And another part of me says no, you will see this through, you will not lose this time. It's like the footsteps are coming not from beyond the door, but somewhere much closer to me. I knew this place would be strange, but all this strangeness is making me afraid, and spooked in an odd way.

Well, what is there to be afraid of? Fear is for people who have something to lose. Haven't I lost enough already? Let Cabbar el Badisi come, let him come as he knows. What's meant to happen, will happen. I'm not going to try to stop anything from happening. On the contrary; I will let it all flow so my life can collapse completely and be reborn.

What is that? The wall suddenly started to open up… It's opening. And somebody just came in… Incredible.

Yes, it's him… Cabbar el Badisi.

The man is dressed in white from head to toe. Is this Cabbar el Badisi? He's around fifty-five, maybe sixty years old, with a pot belly. His head is shaved. He has a beard. He's wearing small earrings that are shaped as number zero. I would say they are hoop earrings but they're not; they are zeros. He has something like a shawl wrapped around him, and he's wearing white pants. Was I expecting someone like this?

Here comes this strange man… This is the man who is going to save me, Mr. Cabbar!

His eyes are so strange… It's as if there are two small balls of fire coming out of them. What about his nose? His aquiline nose is so charismatic. He's not a particularly good looking man, but it's almost like he is going to swallow me up entirely with his energy. Not just me, but this entire building. In fact, I feel like he can

51

absorb İstanbul entirely with this energy.

It's like I'm caught inside a storm. I'm engulfed in a very powerful energy. I can't move. I'm already under the influence. Good, I have just come to the right place. Now I have no doubts left.

"Welcome, Miss Berrak. Here, let me get you seated over here, on this side of the table."

I realized just now that on top of his shaved head, he's wearing something like a kippah… But no, it's not exactly a kippah; it's a small cowl adorned with strange and colorful symbols, and signs that I have never seen before. I had never seen a cowl like this one before. But if you pay attention, you can see that it is a cowl. Is he wearing that shawl to add more mystery to the occasion? If that was his purpose, he has certainly hit the nail on the head.

I wasn't expecting someone like this; I though he might be gaunt and entirely dressed in black. I thought he would be older. He has an interesting face; he looks like an endearing person from the side, but who would believe that considering his line of work? However, when you face him directly, eye-to-eye, he's scary. Like Mona Lisa. His face is simultaneously both very dark and very light. Two different expressions share one face at the same time. This is truly rare… I can't keep my eyes off him. I'm blatantly staring at the guy, he's going to feel uncomfortable. I wonder if he can read thoughts too? Maybe he can; after all, Mr. Cabbar is a very special person. It would be strange if someone like this couldn't read thoughts. I bet he can. Ugh, it's suddenly so hot, is the air conditioner not switched on? Does this room even have an air conditioner? I might pass out.

"I'm sorry Miss Berrak, we cannot have the air conditioner switched on during sessions. You will just have to bear the heat."

Alright then, he can read my thoughts. Then he knows what I think of him.

"So, how do you like my office, Miss Berrak? Is there anything in here that seems familiar to you? Your eyes tell me that you find me and my clothes to be rather odd. As if you were expecting to see someone else. I suppose you have pictured me differently in your head. What were you expecting, Miss Berrak? Someone dressed as a surgeon, or a butcher? Or did you assume I would be carrying a cauldron? A wizard's cauldron… A hook-nose. Although my nose isn't too small as it is, ha ha ha ha… I think that's what you were expecting. Oh, you make me laugh, Miss Berrak. And may God make you laugh in return. Or were you expecting to see someone clad in black leather and metal accessories? Or someone in a murderer's outfit? Would you mind telling me, Miss Berrak, what exactly is a murderer's outfit? What do killers wear? People have such preconceived images and templates of what things should look like. That makes me laugh as well. As if bad people have a particular way of dressing themselves. Malignancy and evil have been stereotyped in very specific ways in people's minds. The same old stories are repeated on tirelessly. "Malicious people wear black." Well, there is no such thing; they can wear whatever they want, whether it's pitch black or crisp white. And all the horror movies and thrillers feed off of these cliches. Obviously symbols are important, as you can see, I use them too. However, Miss Berrak, the truth is that 'Evil wears no costume, but if it did, it would wear the costume of the good.'

Some symbols and names are surely important, but you must remember that we live in a time in which symbols and names can be distorted. In fact, the world has became a place in which all the symbols have been hollowed out, stripped of all meaning, specifically to create confusion. For example, Miss Berrak, you have a beautiful name. And do you think your name matches your character? Do you carry the meaning of your name as a personality trait? Are you truly so open and visible? Are you as clear as a drop of water? I doubt that, you did come here, after all. This is place is not brimming with transparency and purity. On the other hand, you do have a point. Symbols have been hollowed out. Although I never do that. Everything I use is real. Rest assured; if the intention is real, then so will be the outcome. In fact, it all comes down to the intention, Miss Berrak. If there is no powerful intention, then no procedure can lead to success. Although I do not deny my own skills. Even in cases where the intention is inadequate; amongst those who come to Cabbar el Badisi, not a single person has faced disappointment. Would they be calling me "The Malicious One" if I were to disappoint my clients, Miss Berrak? There is nothing worse than a failed attempt at malignancy. I'd even choose good over failed evil… Ha ha ha!"

Oh my God! He's a terrifying man and he's reading every thought that crosses my mind. He has answered all the questions I had been thinking of. Nevertheless, I have another question for him to answer.

"I see, but what about the swastika?"

"The swastika… It is beautiful though, isn't it? You see, this swastika I have here exactly two hundred years old. It has antique value. Perhaps you lack certain knowledge in this subject, Miss Berrak. Perhaps you don't quite know the meaning of swastika. Swastika is a Sanskrit symbol and its actual meaning is 'to be well'. The swastika is seen as a sacred symbol in many cultures. Hindus and Buddhists deeply care about this symbol. It had been sacred for the Mayans, too. The four arms represent cosmic power.

Fire, air, earth, water. So, the four elements. There is also a fifth element; ether, or space. In our world, everything has been created with the four-elements principle but people don't even see this simple knowledge that stands right before their eyes. Such is their blindness and foolishness. Those who see that the masses are blind and foolish, rule over them. Those who claim that the masses are not blind nor foolish, get ruled. The truth is as clear and plain as that, Miss Berrak. As I have said, the swastika means to be well. And what happens when you flip the swastika to the opposite direction, Miss Berrak? This shouldn't be hard for you to guess... This is why Hitler used the flipped swastika. Straight or flipped, the swastika always remains as a powerful symbol. Yes, it's true, you can also perform sorcery with this cosmic symbol. That just happens to be my job. And obviously, my swastika is also flipped. It's not as if I would have any other way.

They say the swastika hypnotizes people, and it is said that Hitler chose the swastika as the Nazi symbol to hypnotize the masses. And it's true; he did. Of course, he used the flipped version as well. As for colors, he chose black over a red background or used other combinations consisting of contrasting colors. You see, red is the color of aggression and war energy, in other words, it is Mars. Black is both Mars and Saturn. Classical astrologists claim both planets to be evil, or malicious; but that would be an unfair classification. Without Mars, the energy that drives us to fight in a moment of peril, how would we survive? Plus, Mars rules sexual energy. Do you have knowledge on astrology, Miss Berrak? I assume you are a Scorpio. The bright and profound gleam in your eyes give it away. In any case, one must have a Scorpio accent in their chart for them to come here. Scorpio is ruled by Mars. Scorpios are vindictive. So much so that they end up stinging themselves. I have mentioned that Mars rules sexual energy. Venus is erotism, Mars is pornography. Both are essential for sex. For a true sexual feast, Mars and Venus—meaning, erotism and pornography—have to unite.

Symbols aren't all bad, Miss Berrak, it's the way you use them that makes all the difference. These are all lengthy subjects. You can come over for tea some other day and we can talk them through in detail; but now we have work to do.

Although you must admit, they are truly impressive colors. Are you impressed? Ha ha ha ha ha…

If you must know, I am not a Hitler fan. As you know, I'm interested in smaller changes, smaller malignancies. Although I do contribute in mass evil every now and then; provided that there is demand! But we don't do those things on our own, we collaborate. Union is strength, isn't that so? There are many international organizations that work with evil energy. You can not begin to imagine the sort of energy exercises and re-directions they use. Businessmen and women of sound mind and of certain age, bureaucrats, aristocrats, titans, jurists, doctors, financiers, media moguls, actors, broadcasters, politicians: they are all involved in this energy business. You could never tell by their appearances, they all seem perfectly respectable and principled. When many energies unite, it produces an impressive result and so, it makes it very easy to alter the perception of the masses. If you can change perception, you can change anything. Yes, I have been involved with some major organizations; your eyes tell me you are curious. Miss Berrak, you are smart enough to understand that nothing in this world is what it seems. Heavy is the head that wears the crown. It's all hidden in the intention within the desire to decide for somebody else. The seed is planted by the wish to rule somebody else, whether you aim to do good or bad. Because that wish means you see yourself above that person; that you feel like you are entitled to more rights than them. This is exactly where it begins... The self-help people call it ego. It's actually *nafs*... One of the greatest manifestations of *nafs* in our world is money. What's done is done when money begins to rule over you instead of the other way around. Money is never actually just money, Miss Berrak; money is energy. But truth be told, it is my favorite kind of energy... Ha ha ha ha ha.

On the other hand, mass perception alteration and such aren't very difficult, but I prefer to run my business on a face-to-face basis. The darkness within one person is always more intriguing to me. Because everything begins with one energy, and that one seed. I didn't know you found symbols so interesting, Miss Berrak. As it turns out, we have quite a lot in common.

If you are looking for a symbol, how about the ones over there, on the wall? I believe in just one symbol: yin and yang, male and female, bitter and sweet, dark and light. That good and bad are all one and the same. That choices are made by free will."

"Muhteşem had mentioned that you have relocated from Morocco to Russia. Was it very difficult for you as a child?"

Cabbar el Badisi went silent. It felt like everything else had gone silent along with him, too.

Everything in this room. In fact, everything in the whole world.

It's a profound, eerie silence. It's so silent that it feels as if time stops. As if we are forever in the same moment. Even the thought of being stuck in one moment is too terrifying. What if it's an unpleasant moment that you're locked in? But aren't we all locked in a moment, even if it's not as real as this? I still live in the moment that I broke up with Kerem. I can't leave that moment. I'm always in that moment. But now, the moment I am locked in here with Cabbar el Badisi, is terrifying. I feel a cold chill running down my spine. I started to tremble. I wish I hadn't asked him that question. Right after I asked it, this unbelievable energy manifested itself. His eyes are so profound. It's like they can penetrate through all the dusty, dark corners of the past… He's about to tell me something, I can feel it. He's going to tell me something about his own heart. But why? I feel like this strange man and I have formed a deep bond. Like he and I have something in common. A longstanding bond that shapes our lives.

"So, my childhood has caught your interest, then? You aren't the kind of person who would be contented with what is seen by the eye, either. I have piqued your curiosity. I knew it… Marrakech was were I was born. All of its streets were where I was born. All of its smells were where I was born. Because my mother was there. She had pitch black eyes like those of a gazelle. She never needed to wear kohl around them; her eyes naturally looked like she had worn it. She had thin, soft arms, adorned with gold bracelets. She had long, curled eyelashes. My mother smelled so good that her scent would light up my whole life. I have never caught her scent again in anywhere on earth. In no woman. I have known many women, and I have been all around the world. My mother was very young. She was seventeen when she gave birth to me. And she died when I was five years old."

"I'm sorry to hear that, Mr. Cabbar. That's a terrible loss. It's beyond description. I'm all too familiar with loss. My father died when I was quite young, too. I lost him. And along with him, I lost a part of me."

"I know, Miss Berrak. I know everything about you; as you see, I'm good at my job. That is partially why I feel sympathy

58

towards you."

"Your mother's death must have devastated you, I assume you went to Russia after that."

"The way she died as much as her death… My mother was twenty-two, and my father was sixty-four years old. My father choked my mother to death in a fit of jealousy. Whereas my mother had no fault except being young and beautiful. I was playing out in the street, and I ran back home to find my beautiful mother's lifeless body. My father had left the house. My beautiful mother had left me. My mother, scented with jasmines. She was laying silent and still. I screamed out. Along with that scream, I ripped out all the goodness in my heart. That scream drew all the curtains within me wide open. After that, I could see everything. Over time, I realized I could do more than just see. I would later find out that I possessed some strange power which enables me to shape events however I wish. I was later taken in by my maternal grandfather Raşid, who gave me over to the Russians after some time. He was right to do so. We had no money and he was afraid of my father's malice. In any case, I never wanted to see my father again. I no longer wanted to live in that place without my mother. For me, the life that had began there, had came to an end. When I was seven, I went to Russia with Irina and Ivan, which turned out to be much better for me. Irina has sort of raised me—if you could call it 'raising', that is. Miss Berrak, I'm only telling you all this because you asked. That's all in the past now. I love my job and I think I'm very good at it. After all, that's why you are here. You can rest assured that it will be done to perfection."

He's hurt, too. He's hurt, just like me. He has lost his mother. And at such a young age, too.

He does malicious things, he destroys people's lives, but he has a pain inside him too. How strange... Maybe he lost all the goodness he had in him on that day. Maybe he was transformed then. A scene from one of the Star Wars movies comes to my mind—almost as if I'm living that scene while speaking to Cabbar el Badisi—Anakin Skywalker's story before he became Darth Vader. Yoda had said to little Anakin who had lost his mother: "Fear is the path to the dark side. Fear leads to anger. Anger leads to hate. Hate leads to suffering."

He was almost a different man when he was talking about his mother. Someone you could even love. I felt like I got a glimpse of that young boy inside of him, who had been hidden away in a dark cave for hundreds of years. Desperate, sad, all alone. Unloved. But then he changed back to his usual self. His voice became commanding again. The energy changed. And now, his gaze is back to normal. He has an energy that completely dominates over whoever he's addressing. He has such a way of ruling over you without doing anything, you find yourself captured by that odd darkness in his eyes and that deep tone in his voice. I feel like the eight of swords from the Tarot: hands tied up, eyes blindfolded. His absolute power in dominating is truly frightening. His power stems from somewhere far too deep inside. Far, far too deep. Which is the case with all true power. From the lightness or darkness of the heart. Sometimes, it's from both. And for people like me, from the purgatory of the heart.

Muhteşem had mentioned that he is a very strange person, but no matter how many times you are told, you can never exactly picture someone like this. Although I was curious, my issue was never Cabbar el Badisi's personality. I have one issue, and that is Kerem. And there is only one person whom I believe in, and that person is Muhteşem. Muhteşem exclusively tells the truth, and he knows what's best. Muhteşem is a very special person to me. He's irreplaceable.

Yes, that is Muhteşem… Muhteşem is the smartest, most sensitive, loneliest, most special person I have ever met. He has been written into my destiny and I have been written into his. He and I have been together ever since we were infants. We were born two months apart: I'm a Scorpio, he's a Capricorn. I was born on the nineteenth of November, and he was born on the nineteenth of January. Two months. Not even off by one day: precisely two months.

He is my dear cousin, my other half. He's the youngest son of my mother's uncle. We are related, but not on the first degree. My mother and her uncle are only seven years apart. I call him uncle for that reason, along with not having any real aunts or uncles of my own. So technically, Muhteşem's father is my great uncle. But we were very close as a family, so we grew up together.

Muhteşem is the male version of me. My ugly, freak of a soul twin. My beloved, ugly, hunchbacked cousin. I'm the one he's closest to, and he's the one I'm closest to. I'm the completely lonely daughter of a father who was weak in the face of women, the world, and life, who eventually drank himself into an early grave; and a mother who is full of hate towards men, the world, and life. But Muhteşem has always managed to eradicate my loneliness. He was always the one to do that.

In school I had Murat; but through my whole life, it was always Muhteşem who was truly by my side.

We grew up together. When we were kids, Muhteşem and I would play games for hours. They were all make-believe games. He was frail, weak. We couldn't play outside. We couldn't run. I could climb up a tree whereas he couldn't, I could run around whereas he couldn't, I could skip and jump around whereas he would just have to sit down and watch me do all those things. So he and I had to build a special world of games—a game country whose language was unknown to anyone else but us two—and so we did. This land had some dark dungeons and scary tunnels; but it also had tunnels of love. It was situated between wonderland and freakland—right in the middle.

I would always be the princess and he would always be my slave. I would tie my mother's scarves to one another and tie one end around his throat. I would drag him across the floor. I would make him my slave, my horse. I would pause occasionally to see if he was pleased to be my slave or not. The look on his face was always somewhere in between. Obviously a part of him was content; because we had built a special world in which only us two existed in. No third person could enter this world. We were kids, we would laugh a lot. I would get us ice cream, and we would laugh loudly as we devoured our chocolate, strawberry, and walnut ice creams. We would shriek. Muhteşem might have been incapable of jumping or skipping; but he could certainly shriek out. We would compete over who would let out the scariest shriek. I don't know if screaming disperses a different sort of energy, but I know with certainty that an odd energy would rise out of Muhteşem when he screamed. He would always win at this game. I can let him win this one at the very least, I would think to myself. He has already started his life with so much loss. We would have so much fun together. Muhteşem made me experience the joy, ease and security that comes from being loved unconditionally. The pleasure and safety of being loved unconditionally, forever, with no risk of being abandoned. It was a divine feeling. The odd assurance of somehow knowing that he would love me as long as I existed; of knowing I would never be alone as long as he existed. What Muhteşem and I had was like a morbid but fair deal that was made with God. Like buying your gravestone before you die. You know it's dark and creepy, but you also know it's yours forever.

I loved him, too. Of course I loved him. Not the way I would love a man, obviously, but he was my ugly duckling. My weirdo. What he and I had was a creepy kind of love that I couldn't exactly name or describe or perhaps, didn't want to describe. Who knows, maybe love has uncharted territories. Maybe it comes as a different kind, a different color. Maybe love is just two solitudes, saluting each other.

What presents destiny has to offer to you, or what it may take away from you; details of what it has planned for you is sometimes determined before you are born, and sometimes after. You just know from the beginning that some people are off to a good start. The first outline of your destiny is built by your family, its financial situation, and social status. When you're off to such a good start, you assume everything's alright. That's the presupposition. But sometimes, unexpected things happen and it completely disrupts all your presuppositions. Your trustworthy good start is rattled by a slap from God. This was the case for Muhteşem. Ever since his birth, it was obvious that he would have a difficult life. It was almost as if he knew what was coming for him and didn't want to be born; he put his mother through nearly twenty four hours of labour pains. When he was finally delivered after hours and hours of contractions and intense pain, his mother fainted. I don't know why they didn't perform a C-section. I guess my aunt had some strange revulsion towards C-sections. It may have something to do with her aunt's daughter's death which was caused by complications following a C-section. From what I've been told, my aunt was unconscious for a long time, so she couldn't see her baby until much later.

Obviously, the entire family had rejoiced over the newborn baby boy at first. Because he was the first boy to be born in the family. A boy to keep the family name alive. A crown prince to neatly pass on the genes. As is with all families who are granted with a baby boy; Muhteşem was seen as the heir to the throne by his family, too. A son to keep the bloodline going, to bless the existence of the family. Apparently his name had been decided on from the very beginning: if it's a boy, he shall be called Muhteşem and if it's a girl, she shall be called Ece. I guess they had been assuming that their child would be born as a king or queen; the same way my family thought I'd be clear and pure as my name indicates. Sometimes, life can be very misleading.

My aunt's and uncle's egos had been through the roof. They were pompous and arrogant. My uncle was icy-eyed and supercilious; he had strict principles and military-level discipline. Just like my mother. As a matter of fact, he had graduated from military school. That had played a major role in shaping his personality. Later on, he became an engineer, worked in some top-level companies, and became an executive. Like my mother, he also came from old money. He didn't have any approval or affection for anything other than his own opinions and his own social class. Hating everybody essentially leads to hating yourself though, doesn't it? He was just like my mother. My aunt was not much different either. She would constantly brag about her beauty, her husband, her house, her money. Her biggest dream was probably having a child to brag about. Arrogance was like a sheet that was wrapped around their souls, and it couldn't be torn away. Theirs was the arrogance of wealth, nobility, distinction. Maybe it was the arrogance of fear. The fear of becoming ordinary if they were similar to someone else. The fear of disappearing. They wanted to be different so badly that even their child was born different.

When they had seen their precious son—who had had the name 'Muhteşem' chosen for him even before he had been born—grow up to be a hunchbacked dwarf, they had been devastated. My aunt had never stopped crying ever since she had realized her wonderful child was not so wonderful, after all. Ever since that day, there isn't a trace of her old arrogance. She turned into a person who almost never left the house. She stopped interacting with people. She wiped out her entire social life except for my mother and a very close friend. And my uncle's guards fell. Although he was still known as a pompous man and an executive with great sanction power at his work; deep inside he has turned into a weak, measly, small man.

Muhteşem isn't actually a dwarf, but he's close. He's much shorter than average. And he has a severe hunchback. He is a special person. Within that small, twisted body, there is an amazing brain that lives up to his name. His face isn't too bad; a little disproportional, but you could say he is kind of handsome.

But his eyes… His eyes are beautiful and profound. They are an unusual shade of hazel, and they always shine. Up until the moment I met Cabbar el Badisi, I had never seen anyone whose eyes were brighter than Muhteşem's.

I think Muhteşem is a genius. There are very few people in the world who are as smart as him.

He's brilliant enough to have graduated from both med school and chemical engineering—at the same time. He was born this way due to a rare case of genetic anomaly. Just like Toulouse-Lautrec; that famous, crippled Moulin Rouge painter of nineteenth-century Paris… He had been surrounded by wealth yet he was starved of love, and he died in pain, unloved. Yet he is the first painter to come to mind when Moulin Rouge is mentioned. He had been in the bed of many women due to his wealth, but he had never been loved, caressed, embraced by any of them.

Muhteşem paired his God-given intelligence with an incredible willpower and hard work to graduate at the top of his class in all the schools he went to. When he finished prep school, he was fluent in three languages instead of the usual two. Well, that's Capricorn to you! Capricorns never miss a single step when climbing the ladder of success, and they end up at the top of society; just like a goat reaching the summit of a steep cliff. That had been the case for Muhteşem, his extraordinary intelligence and studiousness led him to the top, which prevented him from being bullied in school. Perhaps there had been a couple of whispers and silent jabs here and there, but by the looks of it, everyone had to take their hats off to him. And he knew. Maybe this was the only way he could protect himself.

I loved Muhteşem in my own way despite everything, and I still do. He is the only man who has never left me, who has been there to console me after every time I've been abandoned. Always speaking in that sweet voice of his to soothe me. My pillow, my electricity.

He was my love slave, I suppose that's always been the nature of our relationship. I always knew he was hopelessly in love with me but we never talked about it. Throughout my teen years and even after, I would always run to him for moral and financial support whenever I was bored or upset. I would take whatever I wanted from him. He has never told me 'no' on any subject. And I always knew that he could never say no to me. I always knew that I was the only light in his dark and lonely world.

When we were teens, I would snuggle up to him, put my head on his lap. He would stroke my hair. As he stroked my hair, I would slowly move my head around his lap to excite him. Juvenility? I don't think so. I was completely aware of what I was doing. Yet I would pretend to be asleep and unaware. I would take pleasure in subtly arousing him. Then I would pretend to wake up and look at him as if nothing has happened, watch the redness spread across his face. His intense efforts in trying to hold himself back and act cool would entertain me. I admired his restraint and self control, I would have loved to see him unleash himself but he never would. There would only be a brief look of pain in his eyes. Maybe that pain ran down from his eyes and into his heart. I don't know. I couldn't give up this game, because constantly pushing the limits of someone who would never get to have me was an unfathomable pleasure. It was good to test it. Testing him, testing myself. Testing his love. Testing how far it would go, how much he loves me, how much he could tolerate me. I've never been certain of neither my mother's nor my father's love for me. My mother had never showed me any love to begin with… I had grown up as a girl who was unloved by her mother. What was supposed to be my deepest bond was cut. As for my father, he chose to leave it unsaid by leaving early.

Then Murat left. And then Cem…

Then who loved me? Muhteşem! I had to know how much he really loved me, that he would continue loving me no matter what I did. Would he stick around no matter what? Even if I caused him pain and misery? What a powerful word, misery. The word itself holds more than pain. It's as if the word 'misery' contains a perpetual continuity. It almost feels like misery is a state that begins at pre-eternity and lasts for ever and ever. A feeling of complete despair.

I wanted to know about all these things, maybe all of it was just a game and I liked playing this game with him. The truth is, I just liked playing a game that I would always win. He has stood strong; despite all my teasing, he has never attempted to touch me. That tension lived on for years, never dissolving and never put to words. Never. A fire would burn in his eyes, and that fire, being desired so intensely would give me joy. Being loved so infinitely and unconditionally by someone she does not desire would give confidence to any woman. In fact, every woman does this. Every woman has a backup. Actually, men do it too. They surround themselves with a circle of attention from their fan base, just to get a confidence boost. To validate their own existence, they give out a constant stream of false hope and keep playing a lighter version of the master-and-slave game. Those who are too weak and too lonely to walk on their own can never let go of their crutches. Perhaps I was one of those people. Besides, Muhteşem wasn't just a crutch to me… I have always loved him in some way. And I always needed reassurance.

Oddly enough, his unconditional love was bringing out the worst side of me. I guess the dilemma between being loved by him, and not being loved the way he loved me by the other men I loved; made me want to hurt him, batter him. Life is built on contrasts/oppositions. His unconditional love made me want to hurt him unconditionally. It wouldn't work, no matter what he did. No matter what… You know how that happens sometimes; it just doesn't work out no matter what you do. It doesn't matter if you give up, and it doesn't matter if you hold on.

Indeed, his love brought out the treacherous, devious part of me. Maybe everybody had a part like this. You don't know until you try. I do not believe in any virtue that hasn't been tried. I know that virtuousness is a state. Virtue is not something you can scatter around; true virtue is not something you can claim to possess before it has been put to test.

You cannot lay down the law claiming you can do without money or make a living the hard way unless you have been tested with poverty and hardship. If you have never lost anything, then you haven't been tested with loss. And if you have never come across someone you can actually cheat on, then you cannot say that you would never cheat, because you haven't been tested.

Am I evil? Maybe I am just as evil as anybody else, maybe I am worse. I don't know because I never tried the others and they never told me the truth. As I have mentioned; there was a part of this that was just a game. But I never told him that, of course. We wouldn't talk much. Both in childhood and adulthood, we could get along just fine without needing to talk too much. I could convey all my feelings to him without talking. As for his feelings; I could never get anything out of him except his love. Because he was actually the most introverted, most guarded/closed off person in the world. To tell the truth, he had had many women in his bed; he was very rich after all, and from time to time he would use his money to fill his bed with women. With "beautiful bodies, empty faces", to quote that Teoman song. With hourly women that he doesn't love.

In his magnificent mansion on the hillsides of Kanlıca, with the sky close above and the sea under his feet, he lived on his own, buried in books… With his cat, Persephone. A black and white, female cat. Well, calling it black and white wouldn't be exactly accurate, as Persephone was entirely white except for the pitch black patch between her brows. I would tease him saying "Your cat's third eye is all dark," and perhaps there was some truth in it. Its name was Persephone, after all.

In mythology, Persephone is the daughter of Zeus and Demeter. Hades, God of the Underworld, falls in love with Persephone. He is so in love with her that he wants to marry her immediately. However, beautiful Persephone turns him down. So, Hades decides to kidnap Persephone. He takes her to his own dark lands and marries her there. From then on, Persephone is the withe of Hades, the God of the Underworld.

I guess Muhteşem's cat was the only thing he loved dearly in this lonely life of his. Who knows, maybe he saw himself as some sort of Hades, too. With the one and only Persephone as his companion; since it couldn't be me. Persephone was just as wonderful as its name implied: it had slanted, green eyes and a piercing gaze. When it fluttered its eyelids, it would give you shivers. It was as if a queen had been reincarnated in the body of this cat. Persephone has never been fond of me. And even though I love cats, I never really liked it much either. I still admired its beauty but I didn't want it near me, and it didn't want to be around me either. I don't like it when anyone can see into me so much, even if it's a cat. Muhteşem was enough for men that aspect, he could see through me completely.

Actually, Muhteşem's intelligence made up for the freakishness of his body. People didn't love him, but they respected him. For instance, he was an excellent speaker, but he didn't really like to speak. He would only speak when he wanted to. His voice was deep and he knew how to make people listen. I have never met anyone who read as much as he did. He had an immense amount of knowledge about anything. After graduating from med school, he got interested in esoterism, occult, and astrology. In fact, he was

70

the one who taught me those terms. And that I was a deadly Scorpio woman. And that I couldn't stop stinging and hurting myself and others. Muhteşem's interest in this wonderful, metaphysical world began when he started learning about astrology. I suppose the actual reason behind his interest in all of this was to find an explanation or a cure for why his destiny was like this, and why he was born with this anomaly. By studying the science of destiny, perhaps he was trying to find the cause of his destiny, and to be the master of it. One day, he had told me that one's destiny didn't begin when they were born. He had told me that the actions or the lack thereof of one's bloodline—up to twelve generations—had an effect on one's destiny. That had made me shiver. Even the lives and stories that we didn't know about had an impact on us. Then which sin was it that I was paying for?

After graduating, Muhteşem announced that he would be doing his residency in Russia. When my uncle asked him why Russia instead of the U.S.A., he just responded with an odd smile. To tell the truth, my uncle's question was absurd; what would Muhteşem do in America, where only beautiful, handsome, young people had a shot? He liked darker places, lands that were partially obscure. But that was not why he chose Russia. Russia was an empire that had produced a monk such as Rasputin, tzars such as Peter the Great, and had made a revolution that could never be matched by any other. And now, it was the center point of all alternative cures. Muhteşem told his family that he wanted to specialize in alternative medicine in Russia. He was going to focus on genes and look for a cure.

It turns out that he had an entirely different purpose in going to Russia. Whilst planning for his residency, he discovered a major parapsychology institute that had been operating underground since the Soviet regime times, and he applied there. He stayed there for two years. But he hasn't spoken a word about the things he has learnt and saw in the parapsychology institute to anyone, not even me. We didn't know what kind of education he was getting there, or what kind of people he had been interacting with. Those two years of his life remained as a complete mystery to us. And I just left it alone. Obviously he has said some interesting stuff, but also glossed over many details. However, one thing I know for sure is that Russia has been good to him. Upon his return, it was almost like the broken little boy inside him had healed a little and he had gained some sense of confidence. He still loved me unconditionally, that much I knew, but I could also sense something different about him. To be honest, I didn't give much thought to this change in him. I did ask him to tell me what happened, but I didn't really insist. Later on, he really got caught up in all of this. He read through the entire corpus of esoterism. He met countless mediums, parapsychologists, and sorcerers. But I remember that he always said Cabbar was the best of all. I was indifferent to both Cabbar and all the other stuff he was talking about until I needed him but today, I need Cabbar more than anything else.

Cabbar el Badisi was amongst the brightest alumni of the parapsychology institute. Two former SSCB agents called Irina and Ivan discovered his talent when he was a child, and they abruptly took him away from Morocco to Moscow, where they trained him. After staying in Moscow for quite some time, he came to Turkey upon the request of the parapsychology institute... He also operated in America for many years. I don't know what kind of operations he ran there, but he was apparently rather high-profile.

Cabbar el Badisi spoke Turkish fluently. It was one of the seven languages he had learnt in the parapsychology institute.

Muhteşem had mentioned that the institute employees operated all over the world, in nearly every country. Muhteşem always called him Mr. Cabbar. This was due to their close relationship, a kind of banter amongst the two of them. As he mentioned himself; I think they are running a completely underground operation. Initially it had started in Russia, but the expansion took place in America. The institute had a massive building in Los Angeles—interestingly enough, the city of angels—which served as an operations centre. They ran everything from there. Amongst their supporters were elite members of the society, wealthy businessmen, artists, finance moguls, men from pharmaceutical and weapon industries, members of the media, top-tier physicians, and even scientists: so it was safe to assume their finances were not exactly sourced from innocent places. Every year, tons of money was funneled to the institute from all around the world. Obviously, it was all illicit money. Muhteşem had also mentioned that the institute had been working on a drug that would completely revolutionize the human immune system and enable humans to live up to a hundred to a hundred and fifty years with no illnesses or any other health problems. On top of that, they also had been working on a system that stops aging at around forty. He had also said that many patients with terminal illnesses had agreed to being test subjects in exchange for large sums of money, for that reason. It went without saying that none of these drugs would be released for public use. The members of the class that could use these drugs had already been selected. One hundred thousand people had been chosen from all around the world. Architects of the new world order. Obviously, the institute's greatest success was in the field of controlling and steering/directing people. And this field was ran by Cabbar el Badisi. He was the head of the institute's HQ/centre of that field, but he specifically chose to work in Turkey. I suppose its geopolitical position was very important for the industry. But according to Muhteşem, there were other, personal reasons why Cabbar el Badisi decided to settle in Turkey.

It was clear that Mr. Cabbar was here to serve, round up more support for the industry and expand its activities further across the world. Apparently, Turkey's geopolitical position from the cold war times still held its importance. It was actually because it was Middle East's gate to Europe. Middle East always had the leading role. No one could ignore/disregard it. It's as if it was the backbone of the world; nowhere else could truly heal until the backbone was healed. In any case, it wouldn't ever heal as long as men like these exist. But right now, I couldn't be concerned with who's doing what. I wanted to get rid of this pain, I wanted revenge, I wanted 100% results.

I needed a real plan, and if the only person who could provide that for me was this man, a malicious one, then so be it. No matter what my dreams try to tell me, I would follow this man. A night before I came here, I had another dream. Why did I always have dreams right before the most important times of my life? Perhaps it was my subconscious trying to talk to me, but with all due respect, I wasn't going to let anything stop me now.

But my mind was flooded with images from the dream. I was walking through a deserted, bare area. I kept walking, yet the road remained the same. I saw my feet taking steps, I saw them moving forward, but the road wouldn't change at all. As I kept walking, a group consisting of different animals suddenly appeared before me. It was impossible for these three animals to be together: a cat, a crocodile, and a deer. The crocodile was belly-crawling. I started to walk towards them, and this time, I was finally moving forward.

Then I saw that each one of them was standing at the entry of a different crossroad and they were all staring at me. It was like each animal was the keeper of the road they were standing on. Pigeons and hawks started nose-diving in the sky above us. Then all the birds rushed in at once. I think there were storks, gulls, crows, and eagles. And a whole lot of other birds, some of which I had never seen before, let alone know their names. Then a very strong wind started blowing. I almost feared its howl would pierce the sky. As the wind turned into a hurricane, I remember a whisper in my ear saying, "Which road will you choose to take?" Subsequently, a very long tunnel stretched out before me. I didn't want to go in it, but my legs were disobeying my brain and leading me right inside. My head and my torso were trying to resist my legs. I was almost about to be torn in half when I surrendered and followed my legs into the tunnel. I woke up soaked in sweat. There, I had chosen my path. You haven't left me any other choice, Kerem.

I chose Cabbar el Badisi. The malicious one. Malianity is like sorcery, but they have their differences. According to Muhteşem; the one who finds, prepares, and executes the most painful of all revenge options is called a malicious one. So, it is a specialty. Not only that, but apparently the plan works 100%. When you go to a malicious one for a revenge plan, he offers you the most violent plan possible, one that can completely destroy the person or people you're targeting. You choose the plan, and then the wheels of destiny start to turn. And Cabbar el Badisi is the one holding the steering wheel.

Yes, I am here. I suppose there's no turning back from this, Kerem. You forced me to come here. You didn't leave me any other option. But we were made for each other. Ours was a very happy and a very unhappy relationship at once, filled with love, passion, lust, and jealousy. I cannot give up on you. I cannot do it.

Without holding anything back,

I have laid my life bare before your eyes.

That is why you cannot figure me out.

Rabindranath Tagore

İstanbul, three years ago, the anatomy of a love

Three years. I have thanked God for every single day of those three wonderful years. Three times three hundred and sixty five days stolen from heaven. Every moment of it brimming with life...

Kerem, am I not your Aslı?

We were prompted by desire, which flashed like lightning between us that night at the party. We decided to get out of there right away. Timur was visibly shocked when we told him we were leaving. Because standing before him were two people who were in love with each other. Timur, who couldn't understand when this love could have started, how we could have been so crazy about each other in such a short time, was frowning. It was as if he was afraid that the party would become dull, that he would have a hard time keeping the other women there if I stole away the most impressive man of the party. He had a point; I had stolen him away. He was mine. Besides, we had been absent from the party for a while now; our feet had been swept off the ground, and we had been elevated completely, separated from our own beings.

We were in the earliest hours of a great love. The earliest hours of a love are like the sunrise in a rose-colored spring morning. The earliest hours of a love are the beginning of a divine time. Yes, we were in the earliest hours, it hadn't even been a full day yet. They were the first moments of love spreading out into the universe... The atmosphere was thick with desire, love, and sex. In that moment, we were only two beings who were trying to ascend towards the sky, freed from all limitations of being human,

79

wrapped up in love, elevated with one another, pushing on the doors of the sky.

There was Kerem, and there was Berrak. The world exclusively consisted of Kerem and Berrak. For me, nothing existed on the face of the earth except for Kerem. I'm sure he would have said the same thing about me if I had asked him. For him, at least in that moment, there was nothing except Berrak. How magnificent was it to be in love.

It was as if our names were written on all the stars. Like the entire universe was chanting our names. Like everything that had been created was meant for us. Like for just one moment, we had never been kicked out of heaven. Like I existed, but also didn't. I didn't exist, he did; he didn't exist, I did. Just us two on the face of the earth. And the world spread out before us.

That night, as soon as we left the party and got in the car, we found ourselves in an amazing shore right outside of İstanbul, where the sea kept beating the coast fiercely. The wild sea crashing on the black rocks kept pace with the passionate nature of our love. The morning wasn't too far away. But the sky was still dark. The night wasn't over yet. The full moon, washing over us with its silvery light, blessed this love like a night sun. I don't remember much about the weather; I didn't feel cold nor hot. I know there was a fire inside me. I was burning like ember. Maybe it would have done me good had I burnt away into nothing. I was being scorched by such an irresistible desire and love. I was looking into his eyes. I was drinking them. His eyes burned with a fire so bright that I didn't need any other light. Our fingers were intertwined. We sat on the shore, side by side. We took off our shoes as we watched the waves break off over the beach. It felt as if the sea, enraged by the full moon, was contesting our madness. I don't know how long we sat there, how long it all took… Maybe it was a lifetime, maybe it was a couple of minutes. But this much was true: in that moment, time was infinity.

The wind picked up its speed, it was tugging on my hair, pushing it into my eyes, and ears. The wind wanted to make love to me too… But now, it was Kerem's turn. Kerem grasped my hair firmly in one hand, pulled, and I felt an immense surge of pleasure as the blood surged into the roots of my hair. Then he laid me down firmly, leaned over me. I could feel his breath on my face. His breath was touching mine. His kiss was like a raindrop on a desert. My tongue recognized his tongue. My mouth recognized his mouth. When he bit my lips, my soul recognized his soul. And then, time came to an end.

That night, another time began. Our time.

After that night, we were never apart from each other. We couldn't be even if we wanted to. My thirst had finally been quenched. My journey was finally over; I had reached the harbor. I felt like I had finally found my other half. I was no longer lost. I had Kerem. I was no longer alone. I had him. There was a man who loved me fiercely. I had every night in which we made love passionately. From that moment on every morning was a summer morning, every night was a summer night for me. I was right in the center, in the heart of a happiness I had never known before.

Even greater joys would come along later. Before long, he suggested that we live together. I was bursting with happiness. My savior had arrived. Finally, my knight who would save me from my cave of eternal misery, from that gloom I had been living in with my mother, had arrived on his white horse. Finally, my exile was over. After I met Kerem, I hadn't really been going home too often anyways. Piece by piece, I moved my furniture into his house at

Yeniköy. The less stuff I brought along, the better. I didn't need too much anyways. On those first days of us living together, I was so happy that I felt like all those dark feelings and all that loneliness I had been carrying with me since I was born, had vanished. In fact, even my mother didn't seem as horrible as she had before. We just spoke over the phone every once in a while, and things were so much better over a distance. Everything was fine... Except one thing. And that was the relationship between Muhteşem and I.

After I met Kerem, I stopped seeing Muhteşem in person almost completely. We didn't even talk on the phone the way we used to. I never called, and he figured out that I didn't want him to call, so he never called. When I asked my mother how he was doing, she would tell me that he was getting more and more withdrawn from the world. Apparently, he didn't leave the house often. Truth be told, I guessed that he would be shutting himself off from the world. He never wanted to meet Kerem, but I didn't want them to meet either. I had just briefly mentioned to Kerem that I had a cousin called Muhteşem. Kerem was shocked at his story. And I felt like he pitied him, too. But I never elaborated on the topic of Muhteşem. After quite a while since the last time we spoke, I called him to see how he was doing. He sounded just fine, but I didn't need to see his face to know that there was a sad man on the other end of the call. I was a little sad, of course. He had always been an important person to me, after all. And to him, I had always been his one and only love, and one he will never get to have. But what could I have done? There was nothing I could do. For the first time in my life I was as happy as a person could possibly be, and I didn't have the time nor the energy to deal with Muhteşem. Kerem was my whole life. I wanted to be with him all the time.

You know how time flies by when you're happy? That was what happened to us. Kerem and I had been together for one year and my birthday was getting close. For the first time in my life, I was actually happy on my birthday. This was the first birthday I ever had in which I did not curse the day I was born, but felt grateful instead. My first birthday in which I didn't feel alone and lost, but felt like I belonged and like I was complete. Because there was Kerem now. Kerem was a gift for all the birthdays I had ever had.

Before Kerem, Muhteşem would always get me very special gifts for my birthday. The most carefully selected presents I ever received in my bland life were always from Muhteşem. He would always get me something different and extraordinary. Once, he had brought me Aranmula kannadi from India. It was a special mirror that was made by covering the back of the glass with a shiny metal alloy instead of silver. It was only made in the Kerala area in India. The technique was a secret that was passed on from one generation to the next. This type of copper and tin alloy mirror could not be found anywhere else in the world. It was believed to bring luck, wealth, and health to homes.

He had said, "May this bring you luck," as he gave me the mirror.

I loved the Aranmula kannadi. And he had a new surprise in every single one of my birthdays.

That year, on my first birthday with Kerem, I received a package from Muhteşem. Honestly, I wasn't expecting him to get me anything that year. In fact, I wanted him to forget my birthday entirely. As if he could ever forget my birthday. Obviously, he didn't. I had no other choice, so I took the package. Inside it, was a book of Halil Cibran, a Lebanese poet and philosopher whom we both loved.

I turned the cover over. This was written inside:

"My departure was like Adam's exile from heaven. But I didn't have the Eve of my heart by my side to turn the entire world into heaven…

Happy birthday…

Muhteşem…"

Reading those lines sent a cold shiver down my spine. I felt as if I was running in the dark, not seeing what was ahead of me. I was running faster because I was scared, as I was trying to leave that darkness as soon as possible, a shadow had stopped me and dragged me down a darker hole, and I had no idea where I was. I don't know why I was so shaken up by these beautiful lines. Maybe it was because it was the first time Muhteşem had ever verbalized his feelings of love and pain so clearly. We had never spoken up about what was going on between us. Maybe what unsettled me so much was him using my birthday as an excuse to put his affection and longing towards me into words, even if it was through Halil Cibran's lines. I couldn't stop shivering. In fact, I was shaking so badly that my teeth were chattering. The coldness was coming from somewhere deep inside me. It was as if that book had somehow brought along some kind of bad energy to that happy house I lived in with Kerem. It was like something in that book was going to ruin my happy relationship. Of course, I knew I wasn't making any sense, but that feeling had been stuck in my soul. I didn't want Kerem to see that book, so I wrapped it up, took it to the store, put it in some stupid box, and put it away in the attic. That book could not stay in our house. From that moment on, Cibran had to stay away from me.

I was a prisoner of my love. Kerem was all I had, and I was

happy. I was so in love. Even so much as a feather could be an enemy if it was threatening my love.

This was the kind of love that interrupted my sleep in the middle of the night. Searing, passionate. I couldn't ever have enough of him, so some nights I would wake up, light a candle, and watch him as if he was a sacred statue. It was just like that song; I couldn't have enough of his presence nor his absence. I would stare at him and wonder how it was possible to love a person so much. It was like I had found the lost side of me in him. We liked the same books, the same movies, the same songs. Sometimes I would begin a sentence, and he would complete it. We had so many similarities. It wasn't our similarities that was the problem. It was the differences. We laughed at the same stuff. We hated the same stuff. We could understand each other without having to talk. The more I loved him the more I wanted to love him; the closer I was to him the closer I wanted to be to him. I felt like I was lost in an endless thirst. I couldn't quench it, no matter how much I drank. And along with that came the fear of losing him.

What really kicked off this fear of losing was that one night in which I called Kerem, but he wouldn't pick up. Actually, it would be more accurate to say 'triggered' instead of 'kicked off'. I have always had a fear of losing. That fear has been with me almost since I was born. It has never left me.

His phone was ringing, but there was no answer. Not getting an answer to my calls always triggered my fear of losing. Because when you can't get through to someone, when they're not responding to you, it creates a sense of absence. So, the fear of losing had slithered back into me like a virus. With that unanswered call, a small warning signal had been sent to all my dormant pain cells. Although I was trying to console myself with rational sentences, not being able to reach him for almost an hour had evoked the virus of my deepest fears. When Kerem called me later, laughing, I didn't make it obvious to him that I had been feeling this way, but my ear had gone almost completely red, and I was trying to figure out where he was. Even though I said, "My love, I missed you, where are you?" in my sweetest, most innocent voice; I was trying to hold back the severe jealousy, fear, and panic attack that was threatening to make its way into my voice. Whereas he sounded just as he usually did over the phone…

He said, "Well, today we found out that one of our writers has risen to the top of the list, and she was just dropping by the publishing house, so we decided to have a couple of drinks to celebrate. I'll be home in no time, love, it all happened so suddenly."

"Is that so? Tell her I said congratulations… I'm just curious, which book is this?"

"*The Diary Of A Forbidden Love*, it's by Selin Dilcan…"

"Oh yes, I remember it now, love. See you later, then…"

The name 'Selin Dilcan' was enough to set off my alarms. I had seen an interview with her in the newspaper a couple weeks ago. She was blonde with legs that were way too long, and had alligator eyes. With her tiny shorts and ridiculously long legs, she looked like she came straight out of a tabloid magazine. Miss Selin… The writer of a best-selling novel that is adorned with erotic passages. Kerem's publishing house had a sub-brand, Zip Books. Zip would usually publish books like this one; erotic, romantic, based on love or unimportant subjects. The interesting part was, those kind of books sold very well. In fact, it can even be said that these books made the most money for the publishing house. This enabled Kerem to publish the literary pieces that he wanted to publish, but wouldn't sell as much. Kerem was actually very fond of books. This side of him fascinated me. I was always chasing after stories, too… I didn't know why he never considered writing, but he disliked critics. He never wrote, but he was very successful as a businessman and a publisher. Çilek Publishing House was the brightest publishing house in the sector.

The name 'Selin Dilcan', and Kerem not answering his phone for an hour had definitely set off my old Berrak genes. The sleeping snake, which was my fear of losing, had been woken up, never to go back to sleep again.

Actually, there was a fear inside me that was trying to grow as I got closer to him for a while now, I knew it, and finally the black rose of fear had bloomed. I could smell it all the time.

Sometimes I thought that if one of us were to disappear, the fear of losing this love would go away. His love was no less than mine. I knew this, too. It just felt like his love was more corporeal, he loved me in a more worldly way. He loved my beauty and my femininity. And I loved him entirely. And most of all, I loved his soul.

The love I felt for him was so immense. A sly shadow would settle inside me whenever I said "I can live without breathing but I cannot live without Kerem!" An inauspicious voice coming from within me was repeatedly saying "This love goes against the essence of life, a love like this has to end. It cannot stay this high, it will fall." The more I tried to drown out that voice, the louder it would echo inside my head. Fear was gradually taking over me. The more I loved Kerem, the more I became afraid of losing him. I was starting to be convinced that he would cheat on me, that he would leave me. My mind kept producing all sorts of break-up scenarios. I was losing sleep. It was almost like being ill. There was another voice inside me that said: "If you keep picturing so many disastrous scenarios, they will come true, they will turn into self-fulfilling prophecies. Stop thinking about what could go wrong, go live your life, go live this love, own up your man and your love." But I just couldn't stop myself, my mind, my fears. The energy of fear surrounded me. And my fear grew bigger and bigger every day. It was getting stronger, like a volcano that was about to erupt. It was getting strange. I couldn't stop it, and trying to suppress it only made it stronger. I was blinded by the fear of losing him. I was a prisoner of my own fears. I was not myself anymore. Jealousy had wrapped itself around my throat like a rattlesnake. It was like quicksand; the more I struggled to get out, the deeper I would sink. I was realizing that there was no turning back from this. It was lying in and waiting for me around every corner with its somber visage. On one hand, I knew that if I kept feeding these fears, they would come true, and that I would face the things I feared. I was aware that I was getting carried away by my prospectively self-fulfilling fears. But being aware of this was not enough to stop it. The saddle of the horse of fear was not in my hands. I was heading full-speed into the end that my fears were building for me, and I eventually got there.

What followed this was a time of complications, caused by my own self. I was showing all the signs and symptoms of jealousy. I desperately needed a cure, but there was no one to provide it. I had now begun to go through his belongings, and reading his personal notes. With the aid of a friend who could give any professional hacker a run for his money, I had secretly hacked into his accounts to read his e-mails, look around his Facebook profile, track all of his social media, and basically follow his every move. I was carrying out small tests. With these tests—which I would slowly aggravate—I was trying to find out if he was cheating on me. I had become a strange woman; the dark kingdom of Scorpio had begun to rule over me. I was now a Sylvia Plath portrait. When he talked, I wasn't even listening to him anymore: I was looking for the faces of other women in his eyes in which I would plunge into as if they were a dark pond. I was showing up in front of him in inappropriate places. He was always surprised and delighted to see me, but these odd coincidences started to happen far too often. And as the surprises became more frequent, he started to become less delighted to see me. As he slowly drifted apart from me, I just kept asking more questions, and pushing him more when I should have given him some space. Even though the voice inside me was shouting "Acting like *this* is how you'll lose him." I couldn't help it. I was unable to stop myself. A line had been crossed now. It was only downhill from here. So, everything was stuck in a vicious cycle. Inevitably, Kerem began to grow distant from me. As he pulled away, I pushed him more. I began to bring up the subject of marriage. I was constantly talking about getting married, having kids, starting a family. I kept asking him to tell me he loves me. He would say it, then I would ask him say it again. "Will you love me forever," I'd ask, "No matter what I do, no matter what happens, will you love me forever?" I wanted his devotion forevermore. I was asking him to promise me something that was entirely impossible. Granted, had he promised, would I even have believed him anymore? I believe I had crossed that line, too.

His reaction to all of this was to gradually pull himself away from me. The hours he spent at the publishing house were getting longer. Our garden floor house with a small sycamore tree in its garden was no longer our love nest. He came home late everyday. We no longer made any fun plans for the weekends. Around that time, I started drinking more. Maybe having a perfect man like

Kerem whom anyone would want and women would line up for was too much for me to handle. I just couldn't believe that I was loved by someone like that. I thought that I didn't deserve someone like him who was perfect in every single way. Why would this amazing man love a woman who wasn't even loved by her own mother? I also found it strange how everything got better after he came into my life. The store was making more sales. My friends were both envious and respectful of my relationship. Everybody adored Kerem, even my relationship with my mother had gotten better. Despite all of this, my insecurity was growing bigger and bigger with each passing day, and doubts were consuming my mind. The fear of losing him had paralyzed me before I even lost him. Just like kids who would break their favorite toys; I was unconsciously sabotaging our relationship. Maybe I didn't know how to be happy. Unhappiness was something that I had grown used to. And happiness was something I just couldn't embrace. It was uncharted territory for me. Maybe it was my subconscious trying to bring it to an end, since it believed that this would end eventually and that nothing good ever lasted. How strange it was for one's subconscious to play Russian roulette with one's existence.

I was certainly good at sabotaging. Eventually, Kerem had had enough of the third degree and pulled himself away with increasing speed. The more he distanced himself, the closer I watched him. And as I intently monitored his every move, I began to hear the blows that would eventually destroy my happy life as they got closer. I was now fully convinced there was someone else; it was time to catch him in act.

Before too long, what I had been looking out for—or should I say hopelessly feared—came true. One weekend, Kerem said he had to help one of his good friends to move into a new house, so he wouldn't be able to come home that night. In fact, he wouldn't be around much throughout the weekend. His friend's new house was kind of upstate and it was possible that he wouldn't even have any phone reception. No phone reception in these times, huh? Was he actually expecting me to believe that? The only thing left for me to do was to follow him. So, I did. Scorpios are good at following and tracking down. A jealous woman can even outdo the FBI when it comes to tracking. Eventually, I figured out that his friend was actually a woman called Şule.

The woman who was out to destroy my life was named Şule. Şule. An ominous woman whose name began with an Ş. Her name was the only thing on my mind, night and day. The letter Ş echoed in my head non-stop. I was obsessed. Tracking was all I did now.

I began to pore over every single social media account that Şule had. Every day I began my shift; Facebook, Twitter, Instagram, Snapchat… I went through each and every one of them. I sifted through all her friends to the point where even her friends seemed familiar to me. I searched for clues about the state of their relationship in her photos. While I did all this, I was supposedly not mentioning anything to Kerem. I was playing it cool. I had begun losing weight at an alarming speed, because I was consuming myself. My cheeks had sunk in. There were dark circles under my eyes. My immune system was about to fail. It was like I was sick, deranged.

Şule was twenty seven years old, she had studied media and graphic design in England. She was a young woman with many bright ideas. What a woman… She had been hired as creative visual director and was also put in charge of foreign publications to improve the publishing house even further. So she was assigned to two tasks at once. She was a dainty, overly friendly blonde. You know the kind of people who are right for everything? Right for society, for status, for marriage, for being a wife? Şule was one of those people. She had been introduced to Kerem by his close friend Mert. Obviously, he introduced them so she could be useful to Kerem's business—so to say. But I knew he had an entirely different intention. It was clear that Şule was the price I had to pay for not getting along well with Mert, and not making any effort to come to an understanding with him. Or rather, she was the price of taking over Kerem to the point where there was no room left for his guy friends. If a man has never been in love, if he doesn't know how to love or be loved; he couldn't tolerate his best friend falling in love, get caught up in a great passion, and stray away from their manly world. He would feel like their infinite alliance against women has been broken. He would feel cast-out and screwed-over. He would think that he was kicked out of that safe manly world. It would not be about marriage or commitment; it would be the friend in love that would be so unbearable. Choosing a woman as his one true companion and his favorite person is what would break the contract. Because as far as twosome affinities go, love is the least accessible by the third person. This is unacceptable in a man's world. Consequently, Mert couldn't tolerate it, and brought in Şule to distract Kerem. A blonde, docile, dainty woman in the test field of our love. Shiny and new. Compared to me, Şule was certainly more temperate; less passionate, less damaged, less fierce, and much softer. If I were a waterfall, she was a river bank. If I were a forest, she was an English garden. She was born with a silver spoon in her mouth, and all her sharp edges had been smoothed out. Pretty, smart, well-read, but too convenient, too flat, too ordinary…

Mert had done the math well: if Şule came into Kerem's life, then Mert could reclaim his position as the best buddy for life.

And I, along with my Scorpio jealousy and reckless nose-dive into the swamp of over-possessiveness, had already dug my own grave.

All I really wanted was for Kerem to understand all my doubts, stroke my hair, soothe me, and tell me he would never leave me. For him to love me and soothe me as the mother who had never loved me should have done. For him to watch over me as the father who had left too early should have done. I was expecting Kerem to do what Muhteşem had always done: console me and put my mind at ease. I expected him to understand me and love me unconditionally as Muhteşem had done. To accept me with all my faults, flaws, and lost childhood. Since he was the prince of my lost childhood, then it was time for him to kiss me awake from my eternal nightmare. But he didn't. He never said that magic word. On the contrary, he was getting quieter every day. He was just as silent as an ancient monolithic obelisk; and just as full of strange signs.

That day, we were having breakfast. I had prepared him a breakfast that was reminiscent of the Sunday breakfasts of the past. I had intended to set up a table that would make me feel like I belonged to him forever. Happy couples had tables, breakfasts. Breakfast was happiness, it was a beginning; so we had to set out our breakfast table again. We had to start over.

French toast, dill and mushroom omelette, strawberry jam, carrot and orange juice, soujouk, avocado salad, cheese pastries, clotted cream, chestnut honey, and peach marmalade… I had even gone to the trouble of making the marmalade myself. I had put it in an ice blue jar that reflected the light. That tiny marmalade jar was radiating happiness all by itself by sending beams off light all around. That little jar was the lighthouse of the table. Then I placed freshly picked flowers on the table… So the smell of hyacinths would waft through the house. And it did. I had everything set out. I picked a song from the playlist… Adele, singing "When We Were Young". I had gotten up early to set the table with utmost diligence. Then I snuggled up to Kerem, I woke him up with kisses, caresses, tickles. He opened his eyes and smiled. He got out of the bed, stretched out like a cat and walked towards the table. After days, weeks of cold war and a suffocating, thinly veiled animosity, it felt like the house had finally gotten a fresh breath of air. It was as if the war was finally over, the inventory was taken, and a life-long peace treaty was about to be signed on this beautiful table. That's what I had been hoping for. Despite being a Scorpio, I did have the occasional bout of naivety; my rising sign was Cancer after all. Kerem took a look at the table, and he seemed pleased. I thought that maybe we could start over, and get rid of the ever-growing distance between us. Breakfast was happiness; it was to start life with a happy morning. So, who knows, maybe this breakfast would be another chance, a fresh start. I was uncharacteristically optimistic and hopeful.

We were truly having a happy morning. We were laughing and talking like we used to. We were making travel plans for the summer. We were talking about going to vineyards in Sicily. It was like spring was coming to my soul. Like I was in the twilight spring that came before the actual thing. But winter would dawn on us with full force before long. You know how it is: sometimes a meeting with destiny appears before you in the form of a parking situation. As we were dreaming about Sicily over breakfast, the doorbell rang. It was the building superintendent, Mr. Mehmet.

Kerem said, "What's going on, Mr. Mehmet?"

"Sir, you need to come and move your car. I suppose you parked there because it was the only empty slot, but the residents of number nine is stuck behind you now, and need to get their car out. You need to move your car."

And those were the words that Mr. Mehmet used to change the direction of my fate.

Kerem rushed outside. Unfortunately, he had left his mobile phone on the table. It was almost like that text had been waiting for Kerem to leave the house. Click... A text notification sound came from his phone. This was an irresistible invitation for me. I couldn't help but see who had texted him. If I hadn't looked, perhaps I wouldn't be here today. Who knows?

It was from Mert:

It said, "What did you do? What did you decide on?"

Since there was a decision to be made, then there had to be a background to this. So I decided to check it out. I looked at the other texts from Mert. And the conversations between those two shattered my heart into pieces of ice.

Mert: Şule called. She wants to see you again. She said you have to find a way to be with us tonight, no matter what.

Kerem: I can't, Berrak would kill me. Don't you know how jealous she can get?

Mert: We will be at Mekan in Arnavutköy and we'll be waiting for you. Say you have a lot of work to be done at the office.

Say you have a lot of work to be done at the office, is that so, Mert? It's lovely how you're teaching my one and only lover to lie. Destroying my future with those supposedly cute texts... Do you think I'll let you get away with this?

I was shaking like a leaf. Find a way, no matter what, huh? Who did this girl think she was to have the audacity to call out to my lover with these words? How far had their intimacy advanced for her to invite my lover to her arms with such confidence that he would come? He was my lover. Mine. I couldn't let this happen. But at that moment, I was in no state to use my mind and build up a strategy. I wanted to charge at both of them, to unleash my inner beast and tear them apart with my fingernails. My mental state was unwell already; I had just decided to be better again for this morning. But that didn't work out as planned.

Nonetheless, I couldn't let Kerem know what was going on. If he knew that I knew, then I would lose the chance to catch them red-handed. When Kerem moved his car and returned to the breakfast table, I didn't say anything. I was putting a tremendous amount of effort into maintaining my cheerful composure as before. Everything seemed normal, except for one thing. When I raised my head to look at the clock hanging on the wall, I realized that it had stopped. None of the arms were moving. Time was trying to tell me something; it was over...

A song by Model was ringing inside my head...

"But You Love Her..."

Sometimes, life is up against a wall. Even so, you want to break down the wall by yourself. You're your own dynamite. In order to demolish, you need to be torn apart. Sometimes, that's your only choice. That was the case for me. I had no option but to go for the wall.

Kerem had truly been an amazing liar. He said that his mom had invited him, that there had been some sort of a family gathering that he had to join, that all the relatives would be there, that it would be rude for him to not go, and that it wouldn't be right for me to come along at this point. I had met his mother and his sister. I got along just fine with both of them, but according to Kerem, it just wasn't the right place, nor the right time. He was so caught up in his lie, using all his charm to pave the way for his evening fling. It was almost masochistic for me to act like I believed him. It was obvious that he wanted to get to know Şule better. I didn't know how serious this was, and I had to see it with my own two eyes to understand. Even if it killed me, it would be by my own accord. I would not let anyone else to pull the trigger on me.

The night arrived. At first it felt like every second dragged out for hours; and then the minutes just flew by. I had to prepare. First of all, I had to prepare myself.

I dressed myself meticulously, as if I was going on a date. I wore my black high heeled boots, skin-tight velvet skirt, fishnet stockings, classic white shirt and black leather jacket. I applied a dark and smoky eye make-up. I put on a lipstick that was as dark a shade of burgundy as bitter coffee. Since I was going into war, I had to put on my war paint. I left the house to burn that place called Mekan to the ground.

I got in the car headed straight to Arnavutköy, to the entrance of Mekan. I parked the car and took a little walk towards the shore. I lit a cigar, and took a sip of cognac from the small flask I had in my purse. I needed courage. Cognac was to provide it. I smoked my cigar as I watched the sea and continued taking deep breaths. I was having an internal conversation with the ice blue sea and slightly chilling wind. I had come to end a love. I was telling the wind that I had come to end a love. It responded to me in howls, saying "It will pass, don't cry." Yet I cried anyway.

I went to the restaurant, it was crowded. All the tables were full. At that moment, the place seemed like it was mostly occupied by men. A derby game was playing on the gigantic screen ahead. Beşiktaş versus Galatasaray. I was making my way through a crowd of men that were almost spraying testosterone into the air, looking for Kerem. The men had one eye on the screen and the other on my legs, and their attention gave me a bit more confidence. This was good, it helped with my pain. I started to sway my hips slightly more rhythmically, stuck out my chest, and put a Scorpio smile on my face. Half-cynical and half-inviting.

I finally found their table at the back of the restaurant. They were seated in a more intimate spot at the end of a hall. I saw about three or four people, and briskly moved towards them.

There, I had caught them. The table's occupants were Mert, Kerem, and two more guys. But what about Şule? Where was she? She wasn't here... Yes, Şule was absent. They were just sitting as a group of men, watching the derby. On Mert's face, I saw a surprised, yet sly and satisfied smirk. Kerem was shocked. He got up from his seat, grabbed my arm, and started to drag me outside. We were almost flying towards the door. He was squeezing my arm so hard that it had started to restrict my circulation.

We finally arrived at the shore of the ice blue sea and the gulls.

"What are you doing here, Berrak? Did you follow me or something?"

"I should ask you the same. What are you doing here? Weren't you supposed to be at your mother's house? With all your relatives?"

"Forget about that for now and tell me how and why you're here! Are you insane? You just embarrassed me in front of my friends. What do you want, Berrak? I have had enough, what is it that you want?"

"Why did you lie to me?"

"I lied because you turned into a very strange person. You started to get jealous. I'm a man who's keen on his freedom. I can't put up with stuff like this. Am I not allowed to watch a game with my friends?"

"Weren't you here to meet Şule? Just tell me the truth already."

"Şule? Where did you get that idea? Are you stalking me, reading my texts? What kind of weird person did you turn into? You are scaring me. I have had enough of you Berrak, don't you see? You made me grow sick of you."

"I have told you to never lie to me from the very beginning. Never lie to me. Yes, I have read your texts. I know Şule was supposed to come tonight. I don't know why she isn't here but you were surely going to cheat on me."

"Berrak, are you out of your mind? Enough. I can't take any more your jealousy. I'm not seeing anyone. Whenever I tell you I'm going to hang out with the guys you start sulking, you keep questioning me about who I'm hanging out with, I have had enough... So that's how it is now? You're stalking me?"

To be perfectly honest, I was in shock. There was no Şule. There was Mert. It was just a few guys who had gathered to watch the derby. Then why did I have this feeling that something awful was about to happen? My senses would never misguide me. And it they hadn't misguided me now, either. Something awful had happened. I had come all this way with all my overbearingness and jealousy; I had embarrassed him and caused him to be fed up with me. I couldn't let myself get so humiliated. I had only one thing left to do. I suddenly threw myself towards him and pressed my body against his.

"Kiss me..."

Between the two of us, there was the most intense amount of carnal attraction that a man and a woman could ever possibly have. In destiny's plan for this love, in the alignment of its stars, there was an attraction that was as strong as nuclear energy. I was aware of the chemistry I created in him in the past, in the present, and maybe in the future. He created the same chemistry in me. And that chemistry was my way out of this difficulty right now… For a while, he just stared deep into my eyes. He tried to resist my body. He failed. Our eyes were locked onto one another. The moment lasted forever. He was trying to make a decision. He was trying to choose between calling it quits, or continuing. He decided to continue. We kissed. It was like two bodies of water meeting each other rather than a kiss. The brawling flow of two waterfalls. Pouring rain, volcano spewing ashes all around. We kissed each other, again and again. We got lost in each other. Disaster was avoided for the time being. Be that as it may, I couldn't live with all these suspicions. I would find out much later that I had been right all along. Since Şule's father was a member of the football federation, our young lady supposedly loved football games. That night she had been planning to watch the game there with my Kerem, but had to cancel at the last minute when her brother had an asthma attack. So, I had been right, I nearly was cheated on that night, all the ruses and the schemes had been set up, but of course Kerem didn't tell me that. Because a part of him was still madly in love with me.

After that night, several things certainly changed for me as well. It was time for this relationship to come to a result. It had to have a frame that would be accepted and approved of by everyone. I wanted this love to be confirmed by the whole world, by the government, by society and by god.

My mind was made up… I was going to ask him to marry me. It was the only way to possess him. I had no other choice. I knew he didn't want to get married but all other options had been exhausted. We had to get married, or these feelings would be the death of me.

The trust between us had been re-established. With the approaching holiday, there was a long period of time-off. Kerem suggested going on a boat cruise. We would rent a small boat for four days, set sail from Demre in the vicinity of Kaş, and have four days of love. As a Scorpio with Cancer rising, water was my main element, and the sea was my motherland. Kerem's suggestion made me excited like a child, I could hardly wait. Our love was written in water; on the night we met, we had made love by the sea. And now, with the boat cruise, we would be washed by the sea again, and our love would be reborn. I was so happy that I didn't even know if there was a word strong enough to describe it. My feet wouldn't touch the ground, I was in the first hours of love again.

I bathed in rivers, streams and seas that were as bright and cold as ice crystals, and as clear as an aquarium. Together, we flowed with the water, we kissed, we made love. The Dead Sea, The Twelve Islands, The Rock Tombs, The Butterfly Valley, Kaş…

If there ever was a kingdom of heaven on earth, it had been built on that boat. The wind was blowing in my hair, I was at on the edge of the boat in my flowy white dress, and I had surrendered myself to the infinity of the blue sea ahead of us. My favorite person in the world was by my side. He and I were unified; away from all the grief, all the chaos, all the darkness, all the good and the bad of the world. We had simply become one and complete in a blue moment. We had come from water, and now we were becoming whole again in her womb. All my cells were being renewed, they were being cleansed of my dark past, my mistakes, my sins, the things I had and hadn't done. In the heart of the sun, all evil was drying out.

At nights, with only crickets breaking the total and intense silence of secluded harbors, we made love as if we were laying the foundations of the earth. I was secretly praying for him to impregnate me here, in this paradise. I was begging for a baby to grow in my womb here, in this blueness. I was speaking to the stars, the moon, the trees, the hills, and sometimes the birds that flew by in some distance. Kerem had tanned nicely in four days, and with his athletic body, he resembled a Greek statue. He was happy, he felt happy and free with me. Who knows, maybe it was neither Şule nor Meet that drove a wedge between us; it was the city. That dark and dishonest world, the self-interest, the gossip, the envy, the hostility imposed on us by the city. Whereas here, in the embrace of nature, we only needed the sun, the sea, and our love…

At the end of those four days we got back to the city, and suddenly I was hit by a bad energy. The minute I stepped foot in İstanbul, I began to feel trapped in a strange way again. It wasn't just because there was less oxygen; there was something else. I could sense it. But this time, I decided not to give in to this feeling.

For once in my life I was going to say what I felt, and state all the things I wanted, one by one.

My birthday was a couple months away. After our vacation, I had told Kerem that I wanted to get married and have children in every possible way and almost every day. In that boat, my decision to be a mother had became definite. In fact, if I didn't become a mother, if I didn't have a kid, I would be beyond any hope. I told him all of this again and again, sometimes with words and sometimes with gestures.

When we were in bed at night, during our most intimate moments, I told him the same thing again. Kerem wasn't responding. He said neither yes nor no. I was trying to understand his thoughts from his eyes. For the first time, I couldn't read his eyes. I suppose he was in limbo about this decision. A part of him wanted to take that step that would connect us from until death, from here to infinity, which was to father our child. And another part of him didn't want to take this responsibility, and with me, of all people. He was on an emotional rollercoaster, but that was fine, because at the very least it meant that he was giving it some very serious consideration and that made me feel hopeful. I was going to win this war, I was going to be the mother of his child, and we were going to be connected to each other with a bond that not even death would be able to break. If I remained patient and unproblematic, it would all work out, I could sense it.

The topic of Şule appeared to be closed for good. In fact, I thought that he didn't even see Mert as often as he used to. Somehow, he had made the decision to stay with me.

My birthday arrived. Kerem had mentioned that he wanted to organize a nice birthday celebration for me. The best way for him to celebrate my birthday would be by proposing and getting me a ring as the birthday present. This expectation was growing inside me a little more every day.

On that birthday, he was going to take me to Mavi Ay; that fancy new restaurant that was gradually turning into a hot spot for all the upper-crust, white Turks. New as it was, it was already full with intellectuals, high-society people, businessmen and journalists. We had had our drinks at our table under a tree in the half-open garden section of the impeccably chic restaurant, illuminated by the blue lighting; now, it was time for the most important moment. My heart was beating out of my chest, I was wondering if I would become the happiest woman on earth today. Would I finally send the insecure demon that lived inside me back to hell, where it belonged? Would tonight mark the start of a family?…

While I was waiting for a ring, he handed me a bag that I would hate as long as I lived. My head was spinning, it was as if all my cells had stopped living all at once.

He had bought me Versace lingerie as a birthday present. I couldn't believe what he had done. What was the meaning of this? It was an absolutely beautiful piece of lingerie, but I could barely keep myself from tearing it apart and throwing the shreds at his face. Why? Was I not the type of woman he'd marry? Was he trying to tell me that he didn't see a future with me? I felt like I was being suffocated, I just wanted to leave this restaurant as soon as possible and go throw myself off of the nearest high building. This could only mean one thing: we were not going to get married. It meant that we could keep hanging out like this, but that I shouldn't expect anything more. This was him, ignoring me. Ignoring someone was the same as killing them. The energy of murder and ignorance shared the same cursed bed.

What actually happened that night was, an irreparable crack had formed between Kerem and I. We drifted apart like two continents. We were pushed apart by an energy that was like bronze, left to cool. Some wounds could be covered up and left to heal over time, but some would turn into stone with every passing second. On that night, at that moment, that great love was left to cool down. After that, our relationship started going downhill, fast.

This was partially caused by me, because I couldn't deal with the infinite pain and despair within myself. I just didn't know what to do with that sorrow or where to keep it anymore. I felt like I was aching all over. I was right in the middle of a tunnel of misery, and there was no exit.

I started picking fights out of nothing every single day, I made his life hell. I was filled with a never-ending amount of pain and resentment. This road wouldn't lead to anywhere good, I could feel that. But all the brakes that would halt me were blown apart by that Versace lingerie on my birthday.

What we had now was a relationship that was just getting worse steadily. Our love was rolling downhill but neither of us knew how to stop it.

As Kerem drifted further away from home, once I again I had begun hearing the footsteps of a danger which I had been assuming was behind me. That unfulfilled energy wanted to be fulfilled. And that energy was called Şule. Mert had sensed the emptiness that I had been causing in Kerem's life the way a predator smelled its prey, and he took no time to take over that emptiness himself. And he did this with such professional maneuver, that his prey never got spooked at all. All of a sudden, Şule was back in Kerem's life. The fact that Şule got graphic design education in England just made things more convenient. The tale was ready; Şule had been hired to bring a creative, new take to Çilek Publishing House's slightly outdated book covers. That was the best way for her to sneak back into Kerem's life and Çilek Publishing House in a perfectly reasonable way. Everything that I thought to be impossible had all happened, and all at once. Kerem and I were cold as ice towards each other now. We were two strangers in one bed. We no longer made love. The strings that tied us together weren't even tense or thinning out; they were snapping off altogether. I had no energy to try to make things right. I had simply taken up drinking. Kerem either came home very late, or didn't bother coming at all. When he came home, he would find me passed out. Even though I hadn't moved out yet, or the official break up talk hadn't been had, it was over. We both knew it. Maybe not the love, but the relationship was certainly over. If you asked me what would be the most cruel punishment in hell, I'd say breaking up with someone that you're still in love with. The biggest pain. You didn't know what to do with yourself, you didn't know what to do with the rest of your life. It's as they say; it was like death, only no one died.

When that talk hadn't even been had yet, I caught them on act one day.

I saw them walking out of the publishing house holding hands. As they merrily walked towards the car, hand in hand, they found me standing in front of them. I felt my heart break when I saw that brief look of triumph pass through Şule's gleaming eyes. The pleasure a woman who had taken something that belonged to another woman.

Maybe I was evil, but I never stole someone's lover. And if it wasn't for that look of triumph in Şule's eyes, perhaps I wouldn't even be here today.

She was looking at me with a supposedly-understanding look in her eyes, with all the slyness of a woman who was appropriate for the social status, who glimmered like a porcelain vase, who everyone saw as a role model. She had a cynical smile on her face, as if she had seen a beggar right as she was leaving an expensive restaurant. Her feelings were so shallow, they almost fell off her polka-dot skirt and pooled by the heels of her stilettos. No, you cannot take my lover...

I couldn't leave Kerem in that woman's hands. Şule did not deserve Kerem. She didn't love him, I could see that right away. She just wanted someone with Kerem's social status. She would be with anyone who possessed it. If Şule had been a sincere lover, and if what they had was real love, maybe I still wouldn't be here. Or if Kerem could be truly happy with someone like Şule.

That encounter had driven Kerem insane; he had figured out that I had been following him again. "It's over!" he said, "Over. Over. Over."

As plain as that!

But it wasn't over just because he said it was. Kerem and I were together on-and-off for a while. In fact, one day during that on-and-off period, we had one of our best nights so far. Two bodies in one soul, one soul in two bodies. It was obviously a goodbye, and an amazing one at that. Something had been broken beyond repair.

The nature was taking back what was antithetic.

Kerem went back and forth between Şule and I for quite a while. I thought there was no way I could stand it, but turns out there was.

Love has a way of making you do things that you thought you never would.

I had been out of my mind, I had turned into an unbearable person. And Şule, docile and gentle as a dove, had pulled Kerem to her side. I knew it was all an act, but Kerem didn't. Our love was tired, and Şule had assumed the role of a welcoming innkeeper for that tired traveller. She didn't nag, she didn't speak ill of me. As delicate as a camellia, she assumed a position and expanded her land.

Consequently, Kerem was drifting away from me. I could sense that his passionate love for me was no longer the way it was before, and that was the most painful and unstoppable part of it all. For him to not want me as much as he used to. Not love me as much as he used to. Looking into his eyes, and seeing the dream of a stranger.

Whereas love was, as Adorno said, "to come across your own

dream in the eyes of a stranger." I could no longer see my dreams in those eyes.

The distance between us grew as if we were two continents.

And one day, it all fell apart.

All my houses collapsed.

All my saplings died.

He was gone, completely.

It was over, completely.

What followed felt like a never-ending nightmare that landed a fatal blow in every scene. First, he left the house. His own house. I had been out shopping, and when I returned, he had left, along with all his belongings. There was a note on the table.

Berrak, I'm leaving. I'm not coming back. You can stay in this house as long as you want. But it's over. There's no turning back from here. I didn't want it to be like this. I hope you can build a new life for yourself.

Goodbye…

That was all. This note summed up my whole life. You didn't want it to be like this, Kerem, yet it is. Why? We were like a pair of gloves, so why did it all come to this? There was no response. I was all alone in this house without him. I felt like if I were to slit my throat, I wouldn't bleed. I had grown so numb that I couldn't even tell if I were alive. The numbness went on for days.

Then he changed his phone number. He notified employees of the publishing house so they wouldn't let me in. I made a scene. It just made everything worse. He wasn't answering my calls. He had blocked me from all his social media accounts. Even his mother— who always liked me very much— said, "You need to let this go, Kerem doesn't love you anymore."

He doesn't love me anymore, huh?

I was enraged, I tried every possible way to get through to him, to no avail. I guess destiny had made up its mind to separate us, too. And when destiny made up its mind, there was nothing left to do… Except finding another force on the side of the shadows; one that could interfere with destiny. So, I came to Cabbar el Badisi.

Without him I was lonely, desolate, hopeless. I prayed to God for days, weeks, just to hear from him. The silence hit me on the face as harsh as the wall of Berlin. Finally, after a long time, we ran into each other in Taksim. He was standing at the entrance of the ramp that led to Nuru Ziya Street in Galatasaray, past the St. Antuan Church. I had gone outside to pass the time. I bought a couple of books, and I was headed to Galatasaray from The Tunnel. When I saw him from afar, my heart sank. Sweat was pouring out of my entire body. I ran to him, he was with Şule. Our eyes met and he turned his head. As if he didn't know me. My Kerem, pretending he didn't know me. Yes, a brief look of pain flashed through his eyes, but he pretended he didn't know me. Him. The man whose arms I used to sleep in every night. The man whose face I would wake up at night to watch. The man whose scent I would inhale. The man who used to be my lover, brother, friend, mother, and father; was the man who did this to me.

So I was a stranger now? I was a nobody? I no longer existed? I collapsed to the ground. Not once in my life have I ever cried as much as I did that day. I couldn't stand it. I could stand everything, everything except Kerem pretending not to know me, pretending this love never existed. I couldn't let this happen. I was a Scorpio; so that day I decided I would take my revenge. He had said he liked danger. I would show him danger, then. I was going to go to Muhteşem.

The only embrace I could find shelter in.

I got the sense that Muhteşem had been waiting for me. As if he knew I was coming.

In that dark, burgundy-draped shrine of his, with his cat Persephone, he almost knew when I would arrive. On his face was that mysterious smile that I knew so well. He had sat down at the harbor after the storm had passed, and calmly waited for my arrival.

I cried and cried... I didn't have to tell him everything, he could read it from my face. What wasn't written there, he had found out from my mother.

"Do me a favor," I said to him. "If you love me, do me a favor and help me. Help me stop this pain! I can't take it anymore. This time, I just can't take it. I cannot go back to the same life, to my mother. I am sick of being devastated like this. Will you do me this favor?"

He looked into my eyes intently. I didn't know what it was that he was looking for, but I knew that he would help me. He was always there for me, always ready to help. Pulling me out of the holes that I dug myself in was almost like his innate duty. I knew that I was the woman who took over his entire life, I was even closer to him than his mother.

Muhteşem told me about Cabbar el Badisi, what he was capable of doing, and that he was the only person who could help me. Yes, that was who I was looking for, Cabbar el Badisi. According to Muhteşem, nobody and nothing could get away from him... He had never failed so far. If I wanted a real result, I had to go to the best. So I said yes. I was going to all the way.

Time is an illusion.

Albert Einstein

Autumn of 2012, İstanbul, Kılıççiçeği Apartment in Nişantaşı

To be perfectly honest, I still don't know what Cabbar el Badisi is going to do, or how he is going to do it. I'm fine with anything as long as Kerem comes back to me. I don't care how he makes it happen. If I didn't Muhteşem, if it wasn't for him, they wouldn't even let me in here. The man works entirely with secrecy and passwords. As far as a regular person is concerned, Cabbar el Badisi is just an amazing life coach and self-help specialist. He is also providing these services; although I don't see how that can be, the man's main profession is malignancy, after all. I wonder if people see that swastika and those identical, weird plants when they come here during daytime. Or are they welcomed to other rooms?

Cabbar el Badisi is an incredibly impressive person. You can never tell what kind of person he is. No matter how much you look into his eyes, you can never even get the tiniest clue about him. You just feel like you are looking at yourself through his eyes. Despite all the talking, and all the things he told me about himself, I still feel uneasy.

"Miss Berrak, I see that you're a curious person. You know, they say curiosity killed the cat. Don't you ever think about how much easier your life would be if you weren't so curious? There isn't much about me that you need to be curious of. I was born in Marrakech years ago, but Russia ended up becoming my homeland. I have no parents. I was first raised by my grandfather, then by KGB agents. And the parapsychology institute became my

113

home. Then I was invited to U.S.A by some top-tier people. I have done some work there. The years I was in U.S.A were actually my most productive years. I still have some connections. They invite me from time to time and I help them. Actually, I don't really need to travel there. Everything I need is here, inside my mind...

I feel as if you're questioning my talent, Miss Berrak. There are some talents that are innate. I do have them, but in fact, these talents are present in everyone. You know, the universe consists of the same matter, but everything looks different due to differently aligned atoms. I just happen to have a very fortunate alignment...

That's why I do this job... I had to perform the task that I was given in the best way, so I did. My talent improved further at the institute. I've been here in Turkey for a long time. Truth be told, İstanbul feels like home to me. The work field is vast and the clients are plenty. Also, in terms of energy, it is an ancient city. Its historical roots make it a fitting place for energy work. That's where the term 'Byzantine games' stems from, isn't that so? And later, Osmanlı... Ha ha ha ha. I have arrived, and I have built my system. Once the system is built, what's left is application, which happens to be rather easy for me.

Our system is simple. People come to me for me to perform a malignancy which results in their benefit. Of course, I'm not talking about the normal clients. They're just here for personal improvement. I help everyone in accordance to their intentions.

What you intend is what you will get. As I have said before, intention is the essence and the seed of all. The power of intention is great. Every intention has the possibility of coming to life. If your intention is strong enough, you can make it happen. However, people aren't fully aware of this power they possess. Everyone's talking about the energy of intentions left and right, but they have no idea what they are talking about, or how it happens. They just pretend as if they know. The power of intention is greater than the power of atoms, and it has even greater destructive power. As well as healing power. But we create the options.

Now, about your situation… You wish to get revenge from your ex, and as the malicious one, my job is to present to you the revenge options that would be the best for you, and the most painful for him. I can see his wounds, his subconscious; I can find his weakest spot. And you get to watch the results.

I will offer you a plan with three options. We will watch the results together on the screen. Whichever of the three options seems best to you, is what we perform. And you know, it will be without blood, of a tragic scale, and irreversible. So I want you to assume the responsibility and make the right decision."

"May I ask something?"

"Of course, you have the whole hour."

"I don't want him to suffer physically. I want him to suffer spiritually."

"Of course; that goes without saying in the 'bloodless' option. By the way, let me satisfy your curiosity. No, the others—and by that I mean those who don't know about the passwords and the slogans, my dear clients who come to me for my services as a life coach and a self-help specialist—do not see the things you see here, or these screens. As you might have understood by now, it's very easy for me to change the entire decoration instantly. As for the plants; this is a very rare species that grows in the rainforests of South America. We use a highly specialized machine to provide the climate conditions they require, and to tell you the truth, we do spend a lot of money on them everyday. The most important feature of this plant is its ability to absorb and dissolve negative energy. Naturally, a malicious one works with a very high dose of negative energy every day. My body can handle it without any issues, but if it weren't for these plants, you would have turned into salt and ice, fire and ash by now, Miss Berrak. You would be astonished to find out how many people come here every single day to have malignancies performed. Shall we begin now?"

My phone is ringing. Just as we were about to begin. Who can it be? Hang on, I'll switch it off…

While seeking revenge, dig two graves - one for yourself.

Douglas Horton

Fall of 2012,
Nişantaşı, Kılıççiçeği Apartment, before noon.

"Ms. Berrak, are you ready?"

"I am."

Cabbar el Badisi gestured as if he was fending off an invisible butterfly and the screens on the desk suddenly switched on. Yes, that's Kerem. I see him on the screen. Oh God, how I have missed you. It is as if i'm not in Cabbar el Badisi's office and I am about to Skype Kerem. I love you, Kerem, you belong with me. Why did this happen? Keremmmm.

"Kerem Arın, a thirty eight-year-old, athletic, handsome, endearing and well situated publisher. Born in Istanbul but of Rumelian heritage. His family are Macedonian immigrants. Publishes successful books. The owner of Çilek Publishing House, which publishes both literary pieces and self-help books, which is what I do. I can definitely say that Kerem has published socially beneficial works. I am rather sympathetic towards him but don't worry, that does not keep me from doing my job, dear Ms. Berrak. He also plays the bass, rides the bike, supports Galatasaray, plays football every now and then, and is keen on rock music. Currently lives with his sister, who is eleven years younger, and his mother whom he dotes upon. He lost his father at the age of sixteen. He loves a fast lifestyle, and is quite the womanizer. He is tired of your excessive jealousy and overwhelmed by your possessiveness. As it happens, he loved you a great deal in the beginning. Look, here, he is thinking of you, see? Look how happy you are here. You're sitting under the sun. Here, you're at a concert, in each other's arms.

119

Look, that is the sailing holiday you went on, what a magnificent four days you had, right? These are all lovely shots, but they're all in the past now. He has left you, and now has another woman in his life. She is pretty too, and they are happy together as well. Look how happy they seem on the screen. In earnest, a delightful couple, I would say they look good together. Kerem is even considering marrying her. He has grown tired of you, he thinks that Şule can make him happy, serenely and unquestionably. And as he ponders, you want him to suffer. Whereas you wanted to marry him and he was not as keen. He was scared of marrying you, he was scared of committing to you. Look, he is considering marrying Şule, he is not afraid of committing to her, because he doesn't feel deeply connected to her at heart. He is comfortable with her, he was not with you. In fact, he was scared of his devotion and love for you. A man will shy away from marriage if he loves the woman with too much passion. Because a man always wishes to be free. It's not marriage that scares him, it's his heart's allegiance. Because that is the very thing that will make him suffer and render him weak. Men are not as stoic as women, you know that, they do not know what to do with love and the pain that stems from it. They think they will never be able to get back up once they have fallen, and most of the time, they can not. If they do, they are changed forever. They do everything in their power to never suffer again. A way of suffering is to cause suffering. But of course you could not have known that. Because he has never told you. Now, in this moment in fate and life, I will give you three options to choose from, that will make him suffer and you will pick whichever you deem the most suitable. What you must not forget here is that I cannot interfere with his free will. I can prepare the grounds but I cannot make him come back to you by force. I cannot interfere with the free will especially when it is to do with love, although, maybe I can when it comes to different subjects. But when everything is set I do not think that will be an option. Watch me on the screen, and listen to me carefully."

I can kill this man. How he enjoys inflicting pain upon me. I did not overwhelm Kerem. It is not like Şule is paying him. I am.

"I am listening, Mr. Cabbar."

"The first option is his precious mother having cancer. The severe, malicious and costly kind. It will require long-term treatment, the family will be miserable. You know how much he dotes upon his mother after having lost his father. This painful illness will also cause financial loss. His career, no, his entire life will derail. Naturally, this might cause his marriage plans with the dear Miss to be postponed. This will also cause weight gain and hair loss, his charm will wither. How? Let's see on the screen the consequences of this action. Look, here he is at the hospital, look how miserable he is. Look, his career has completely fallen apart. He is drowning deeper in debt. And alcohol problem manifests. He had already been comforting himself with alcohol but now it has gotten out of hand. In the meanwhile his dear sister gets depressed and finds herself in need of psychiatric examination. So, his sister has a severe illness as well. It is as if an ominous energy is completely taking over their lives. Because of the expenses, they are even thinking about putting their house on the market. They lose many bestselling books to other publishing houses. A complete meltdown. A tragedy. But the mother will not die. You said not to draw blood. So the marriage will happen, sooner or later. In fact, this sweet girl will stand by him during the darkest of times which will further strengthen their bond."

"Are you kidding? Of course I do not want that. I like his

mother, as well as her sister, Selin."

"Since you said not to draw blood, I cannot place him in an accident that will leave him paralyzed. Apparently, you were confused while filling out the form. It is rather tedious to cause such a tragedy without spilling blood."

"The second option would be Cenk, that girl's precious ex boyfriend, showing up. They were together when Şule was in university. But Cenk's family did not want her. They sent Cenk abroad to America for his studies. Their relationship lasted for a little while but then they broke up unwillingly. In fact, Cenk started flirting with a Mexican girl and left our precious girl. She was miserable, just as you are right now. Now he is going back to Turkey. He had married the Mexican girl, now they have broken up. He has not gotten over Şule completely, so he will reach out to her. Well, Şule will not say no to a dinner with her first love that broke her heart. What woman can say no to the man who once desolated her, coming back to them on his knees? This particular weakness that women have actually serves me well. I will send them to the voluptuous bar where they first met. They will reconcile. That night, they will sleep together and I will make sure that Kerem is aware of this. He is a jumpy man, he will hospitalize Cenk. If what Kerem and Şule had was true love indeed, she will be able to redeem herself. She might say: "It was a mistake, forgive me!", there is no saying for sure. It is difficult for me to act against love and free will, especially with the template you provided me with."

"I do not want that. I want him to suffer deeper. I want him to feel defeated and broken. I want his ego to shatter into pieces, I want him to feel humiliated."

I want him to tumble as much as I have.

"Oh, Miss Berrak, although it's not always the same issues

that would hurt a man and a woman; rivalry is a crushing thing, I can tell you that with certainty. This goes for both men and women. You could launch a rocket into space with the frequency of rivalry. That's how strong it is. Which is why I will find you a solution that will include rivalry. Simpler, more effective, you say... Let's do some background check on Kerem. Yes, what I'm actually looking for is hidden in his past. His past will present us the real clue on a silver plate. Yes, this is it...

See, this is eighteen years ago, so Kerem is twenty years old here. As you can see, he has been bold back then as well. See how he works out? People who over-exercise tend to have strong egos. Oh, you have no idea how much I love strong egos! I wouldn't be able to find work if it weren't for egos. See, what we have been looking for is just about to arrive... Yes, her. That's the girl. Kerem's girlfriend, with her hair like a black waterfall, the beautiful Leyla. Kerem is eighteen, and Leyla is seventeen. She is Kerem's first and greatest love. Maybe it is due to the name 'Leyla', but Kerem loves her very much. He is head-over-heels in love with her. The word 'love' doesn't even do it justice; he nearly adores her. Leyla kind of resembles you. You have noticed it as well, right? See, her hair is black, wavy, falls around her shoulders. Just like your hair. The resemblance is truly surprising. Men always love the same woman. That first woman who resembles their mothers.

Look, now they are on the second screen, in their twenties, Kerem must be about twenty-four years old. Leyla has gotten even more beautiful. Kerem is still in love with Leyla, but Leyla doesn't seem to care all that much, she keeps some distance. Her eyes wander off... It's as if she's not really there anymore. See? It should have been 'Leyla and Mecnun', but this time it is 'Leyla and Kerem'. And this name is truly befitting of this beautiful girl.

During those days, Kerem is scribbling something, writing, even attempting to make a movie. His biggest dream is to become a writer and a film director. He is supposed to write scripts, make movies, he has big dreams. He truly lives with this dream. In a way, this is a way for him to soothe a longing, because what he really desires is to prove himself. Another one of his biggest dreams is to write the story of three generations, three men of his family, and make a movie of it. This is a very natural desire for someone who has lost his father at a young age. A feeling of completion. He is working on his novel, day and night. This is actually kind of the story of the father he has lost at a young age. Did you know about this? Has he ever told you? Your womanizer, speed-freak man's biggest ambition is to become a famous novelist and movie maker, and to tell the story of his father. The absence of a father leaves very deep wounds in a man's life, Miss Berrak. It hasn't only scarred you; it has scarred him as well… Even though it may have remained unspoken, maybe this was one of the intense emotions that has drawn you two to each other. Some things may remain unspoken, but in energy levels, everybody knows everything. There is no power greater than energy and intention. Money and status pale in comparison… Where were we? Yes, let's continue."

Leyla and I do look quite similar. Is this a coincidence? How can it be? In his fleeting ways, perhaps Kerem was kind of similar to my father. I don't know…

"I knew he was very keen on literature and cinema, but he has never mentioned that he had tried his hand at writing."

"Look, here it is. Can you see, Miss Berrak? He has completed his first novel and first script at the same time. He is nearly twenty-six years old. They are at a party now. One of the most notable people in Turkey, Eren Murat Işık, is also present. That famous writer and director. Back in those days, Eren Murat Işık is a pip-squeak, a bright young man. He and Kerem are close friends, very close friends indeed. When Eren Murat came here from Kars, he has stayed in Kerem's house. They have attended the same school. They have been like blood brothers. There has also been an endearing rivalry amongst them. But Kerem has been more than eager to help Eren Murat Işık whenever he needed, it's like he has declared him as his brother. Here, you will see Kerem sharing the subject and details of his book with Eren Murat Işık. Notice Eren Murat Işık's eyes? They are a bit too bright, like my eyes. Isn't that so, Miss Berrak? He is thinking about something. Kerem's story is based on a boy's venture of into manhood. And Eren Murat Işık is writing an adventure novel, but it also includes a boy's venture into manhood as well. Do you understand, Miss Berrak? Eren Murat Işık is stealing from Kerem Arın. But truth be told, he does have talent, he does write beautifully, and he plagiarizes masterfully, at that. He is also fast and takes his book to the publishing house before Kerem. The publisher finds the story to be marvelous and the book is published immediately.

When the book hits the shelves, Kerem is shocked, depressed. He tells people of Eren Murat Işık's betrayal, but he cannot convince anyone. Actually, he could have filed a lawsuit against him, but he decides to fight Eren Murat Işık instead, and they come to blows. However, this results in Eren Murat Işık reporting Kerem and having him locked up, albeit for a short time. And what happens next? Eren Murat Işık's book becomes a best-seller. It is also adapted into a movie. All of a sudden, Eren Murat Işık becomes the most famous novelist and script-writer in Turkey. Kerem is at a loss. It's as if nothing he does will be enough to avenge himself. He falls into a heavy depression.

What's more, this Eren Murat Işık fellow is quite handsome. Kerem is weary of life, he feels betrayed, he vows to never write again. And then, everything gets worse. That's the way it is; unfortunate events tend to follow one another in rapid succession. Now, watch this part carefully. They are all standing there, see? They are at a cocktail. Kerem is no longer speaking to Eren Murat Işık, he despises him. Eren Murat keeps stealing from Kerem. Leyla is next. He will steal her away. Kerem's favorite person in the world.

To cause someone the greatest pain; you can simply take away their favorite person.

You can see the way he is looking at Leyla. He has his mind set. This game will not end here. He wants to have her. In fact, they have begun having an affair, but Kerem doesn't know about this yet. That is going to change in a moment.

Yes, Leyla has come clean. *It's over, Kerem,* she told him. She explained to him that she was with Eren Murat Işık now.

See how devastated Kerem is? Kerem was done for on that day. A piece of his soul was taken from him, and it will never be given back. Shamans would know this; when someone suffers a deep trauma or loss, they sacrifice a part of their soul to survive. They send that piece of their soul to the land of darkness for the pain they have suffered. They live the rest of their life as a crippled person. A person with a handicapped soul. Of course, no one can see they are crippled, because their handicap is not visible at first. So no one understands that this person, with their wounded soul, can also wound and wilt the souls of others. That person is not aware of the magnitude of their own disaster. That piece of soul that was lost can only be brought back by a shaman. Without such calling, that person keeps losing their soul in the same way a wounded person keeps losing blood. Those who are losing their souls are very easy for us to work on. I'm telling you this to put your mind at ease, as in that sense, Mr. Kerem should be convenient to work on.

Eren Murat Işık is the man who stabbed Kerem in the back over and over, who took everything from him. The man who stole his soul. He takes Leyla away from him; the first woman Kerem has loved, and the one he loved the most. Kerem loses all his confidence. He turns his back on his creativity. He is angry at life, just like all artists that could have been, or those who were hindered. And of course, like all men who have lost the only woman they ever loved to their enemy, he is furious. Like an enraged bull, it's hard to tell where he will charge. His pride is hurt. A tree of hatred grows within him.

He hates Leyla, he hates all women, but most of all, he hates Eren Murat Işık. Why do you think Eren Murat Işık is causing Kerem so much pain? Don't you think it's odd that he has so much hatred towards Kerem? Obviously there is a background to this excessive rivalry between the two but this issue is Eren Murat Işık's private matter. Perhaps he was in love with Kerem, what do you say? Perhaps this relentless hate was towards someone who has been born luckier than him and has embraced him… When we are full of rage, those who embrace us the most are the ones we want to hurt more than anyone else. I won't go into psychological analysis right now, but there is an inexplicable bond in every strange closeness or hate, I can tell you that much. Not for Kerem, but for Eren Murat Işık. As for Kerem, he loved Leyla more than he loved anyone else in his life. He never truly got over that feeling of defeat. His choice of career in publishing, his constant drive to discover new writers, all stems from the desire to create competition for Eren Murat Işık. He has finally discovered and published a great writer, Murat Dir. That broke Eren Murat Işık's dominance on the sector. He feels that he has avenged himself, even if only a little. What I can do for you is make Şule and Eren Murat Işık meet in a nice, romantic setting, and make Eren Murat Işık's publishing house propose an undeniable offer to Murat Dir. Şule and Eren Murat Işık's relationship will break Kerem. He ends up losing to the same man again. He takes up drinking, he becomes a mess…"

"And falls back to my arms!"

"I cannot guarantee that. I am a malicious one, not a matchmaker. To make small adjustments of malignancy. But you have a point; for now, this is the only option that has a possibility of triumph for you. And it's a rather good option, at that. As a side effect, all the drinking might cause him to have liver cancer in the future, that's one of the incalculable outcomes. Or, it would be more accurate to say 'not incalculable, but ignored'. So, what's your answer, Miss Berrak?"

"The third option. It's the best one. I think that one will hit him the hardest. I want his ego to be torn to shreds. The other options would upset him, but they wouldn't destroy his ego. Even Şule getting back together with her ex wouldn't hurt Kerem too deeply. Ultimately, she would be going back to someone she knew before him, but what would make him feel the most defeated as a man would be the third option."

"Correct, Miss Berrak… Clever. Clearly you've been very heartbroken and you know what would hurt the most. If you still haven't changed your mind, the plan will be in action as soon as you leave this building, and the entire arrangement should be active in three months at most. In three months, you will be a happy woman…

So, what's your answer? Do you quit, or do you proceed? I have to ask you for the last time. Because you are about to cross a threshold, and you will experience this with all its consequences. Now, I need you to sign this last part on the form.

"Thank you, Mr. Cabbar el Badisi... Do I need to make an additional payment?"

"No, Miss Berrak. Mr. Muhteşem has already taken care of the other necessary details. Please give him my regards."

"He's in London. I'll tell him when I see him."

"I have a feeling that you will see him very soon. Godspeed, Miss Berrak."

"Alright then, hopefully we won't see each other again..."

"You can make use of my services as a life coach... Ha ha ha ha. I hope to see you again."

He has such a strange laughter. Apparently, he has a feeling I will see Muhteşem soon. Muhteşem went to London two days ago to attend a medical convention, and then he will work at a hospital there. Anyway. I want to get out of here now. Once I pass this hall, I'm out. For a moment there, I thought I was suffocating. If a person can't even be happy when they're taking revenge, then when would they ever be happy? Kerem, you will come back to me. My revenge plan won't hurt anyone. In fact, I will be avenging Leyla for you... But you cannot go back to her, that's not a possibility, isn't it? I forgot to ask Cabbar el Badisi about that. But I suppose that won't be an issue, otherwise he wouldn't say that I would be a happy woman in three months. He's the malicious one, he knows everything. He's supposed to know everything if he's making plans like these...

Oh my God, it has started raining. But it was so sunny when I was on my way to Cabbar el Badisi. The sun is gone... Gloomy...

How did the weather get so gloomy all of a sudden? I feel like I'm suffocating, why do I feel like this? I have a bad feeling. Like something bad is going to happen. It's natural to feel like that when I just left the office of a malicious one.

But there was supposed to be sunshine in me. I should be giddy with joy right now, but I just feel like someone's hands are clasped around my throat.

I have a bad feeling. Maybe it's because of the rain. And it's starting to speed up. I better walk faster so I don't get wet. The rain gets heavier every second, is it going to turn into hail? If only I could find a taxi… God damn it! At this time, they're all rushing to change shifts, none of them are stopping. The rain soaked through my clothes. I can't get a single taxi to stop…

Taxi! Taxi… Oh, sure, once it rains all the taxis are unavailable. I need to cross the street. It would be easier for me to flag down a taxi coming from both directions if I were at the other side of the road. I feel hollow and tired. I'm in no mood to walk, I can barely take one step. I think there's an overpass a little further along the road, there it is. Although the thought of climbing it seems so impossible right now. Damn it, why aren't there any taxis here? I might as well run across the road to get to the other side. It's a little dangerous but I'll be fine. I'll be quick. I can't climb all the way up the overpass for the life of me. Come on Berrak, just run across.

Oh my God… That car came out of nowhere. And it's coming towards me really fast! Stop, you're going to hit me. Stop… Stop!

"There's been an accident. Get out of the way. A car has hit a young woman. She's laying on the ground. She's bleeding a lot. Someone call an ambulance. I think she's dying, the car must have hit her hard… She's losing blood. Quick, call an ambulance…"

I think they're talking about me. Everyone's hovering over

me. I want to tell them to back off, that I cannot breathe; but I don't think I can make any sound. I was crossing the street. My stomach feels so warm. And my hands are sticky… Is this blood? Yes, it's blood. Oh my God, have I been injured? But I can hear everything. Am I just going unconscious, or am I dead? Dear God, what has happened to me? The car was coming towards me so fast…

"Hold on, I'm a doctor and a family member of the injured, may I?"

But I recognize that voice. It's… It's… Muhteşem's voice. It's him. But how could that be? Wasn't he in London? He told me he was going to London. But Cabbar el Badisi told me to give his regards to Muhteşem. I told him he was in London, but he told me that he had a feeling I'd see him soon. He was right, after all. It is Muhteşem's voice. How? He has come to save me. Once again, he's by my side. Good God, he has come to save me. I have to talk to him… He will save me, he will save me again, just like he always does. I'm so thankful for his existence. He's always there.

"Oh my God! Muhteşem, is that you? I'm hurt. I can't move. I'm bleeding out. Help me. Save me. Please, help me. I'm so glad you're here. But what are you doing here? Weren't you in London? Do you know what happened? I couldn't find a taxi. I had to cross the street. I had just left Cabbar el Badisi's office. I had to…"

"Sssh, don't speak, sweetheart. Save your energy. I know you were just leaving his office, I'm the one who sent you there, remember?"

"Muhteşem, it hurts so much. It's like I was tossed by the impact of the car."

"Don't you worry, dear. I have called in an ambulance, and it should be here any minute now."

"Muhteşem, I think I'm dying. It hurts so bad… I don't think the bleeding is stopping."

"Don't worry, sweetheart. You are not going to die."

"I know you will save me. I'm not going to die, right? I'll get better."

"No, lover, you are not going to die, would I ever let that happen? Would I ever let you die? You will just slip into a heavy coma soon. Your eyes will close, you will be in a deep sleep, and I will be waiting by your side the whole time. Then you will heal, slowly. You will get better, you will be beautiful again. I will always be by your side. From now on, I will do everything for you. I will push your wheelchair, take you to meadows, to the sea. I will give you baths."

"What do you mean, 'I will push your wheelchair, give you baths'? Muhteşem, what does that mean?"

"Because you will be crippled, my dear. You will never be able to walk again. Thereby, you and I will be equal. I will take care of you, and we will never be apart again. In three months, you will be a happy woman, Berrak."

"Oh my God! Muhteşem, did... did you? But... was it you?"

"Yes, baby, it was me. When you choose malignancy, you cannot predict the outcomes. You step into a road of no return. And you can never know what is it that you have called upon yourself. I have outsmarted you. I told Cabbar to make it bloody and irreversible."

"How could this be? How could you do this to me? You, of all people! You, who always loved me and wanted me to be well!"

"Do you remember what Cabbar el Badisi had said, my love? 'Evil wears no costume, but if it did, it would wear the costume of the good...'"

THE END

132

PERHAPS THE END IS NOT THE END...

If you remember me, then I don't care if everyone else forgets.

Haruki Murakami

Autumn of 2012, İstanbul, Kılıççiçeği Apartment in Nişantaşı, before noon, parallel reality

My phone was ringing. Just as we were about to begin. Who could this be? Hang on, I'll switch it off…

In the universe, sometimes a gap appears inside a moment. That gap is a vibration in which everything is formed, and all things are possible all at once. In this state of jumping from one possibility to another, there is no absoluteness of neither time nor person; the moment is just a vibration. It cannot be seen by the eye, nor felt by the hand; it is a transition that can only be sensed. And now, in that transition… Within the same moment, once again…

"Are you ready?"

"Mr. Cabbar, just a minute please, I have to take this call. May I have a minute?"

"Miss Berrak, I think we should get this done first. Then you can take calls as you wish."

"Mr. Cabbar, please, I need to be excused for a minute."

"I'm telling you, it's better if you don't."

"I thought I had my phone on silent, but it just rang. But it is still on silent mode. I wonder how it could ring? How could I hear it? Nevertheless, I did hear it. See, it's still ringing, I can hear it. This must be a sign, I have to take this call. My gut is telling me I should take it. Plus, you cannot pressure me like this. I can answer my phone if I want to."

"I am not pressuring you. However, I am telling you not to take that call."

"What about free will? I thought you could not interfere with free will. Right now, you are trying to restrain my free will. I am going to take this call."

"I am not trying to restrain anything. But since you came here by your own free will; you have signed the forms and stepped into a road of no return."

"No, I haven't. I haven't fully agreed yet. Also, your secretary mentioned that there was an option present in case I changed my mind. Even if I had signed everything. The final word has not been said yet. You need me to say 'Okay' to be able to start the procedure. It was written so on the papers. So, I'm going to answer my phone now."

I can't believe this... It's Kerem... And he has called twice! And he has sent me a WhatsApp message, too. Oh my God. After all these months, he texts me. Not only that, but he texts me on WhatsApp, which was where he had blocked me first. Good God, I can't believe this, how can this be? I wonder what the text says. It can't possibly be anything worse than what has happened so far. I wonder if he has texted me to tell me he's getting married to Şule? Or some other awful event? What more could it possibly be? God, I feel like my heart stopped in infinity.

Berrak, I have called, but I couldn't get through. So I'll just write it here. To be honest, I don't exactly know what to say. In a nutshell: I don't think I'm happy without you, I have never been. Şule and I are not right for each other. I just realized this today, all of a sudden. All I know is, I just miss you. I don't know if you can ever forgive me. Come back to me, let's start over. Let's get married.

What in the name of God is this? Kerem is coming back to me. He broke up with Şule. He realized Şule wasn't right for him. And all of this is happening right when I come here to curse this love forever. What is the meaning of all of this? Kerem... My Kerem. He finally realized that he loves me and not her. Dear God, thank you. He embraced this love, our love. He wants to start over. He wants me. He never got over me either. Our love has beat the darkness. We are soulmates.

Well, what am I supposed to do now? How do I get out of this place? This cursed place. Is Cabbar el Badisi just going to let me go? Will I be able to cancel everything? No, I do not want revenge. How could I even think of harming Kerem in any way? How could I ever imagine destroying the man I love? Dear God, how blinded was I by my own anger and darkness that I came to a malicious one? How could I ever do this? How could I ever stoop so low, become so dark and evil? It's like I just woke up from a dream. Well then, will I be able to get out of this bog? Is there salvation for me? Good God, please help me, what do I do now?

I don't have anything to do with this place anymore. I have to get out right now. I have to cancel all the agreements. I even have to wipe the memory of ever being here from my mind.

"Mr. Cabbar, I'm cancelling the deal."

"Miss Berrak, did you think this through?"

"Yes, due to some news that I just found out, the deal is no longer necessary, but you already knew that, didn't you? That's why you tried to keep me from answering my phone."

"Everything begins with an intention, Miss Berrak, as I have told you before. But if you think you can get out of this so easily, you are mistaken. A big arrangement has been made."

"Yes, and I signed it, but one last signature of approval was necessary, and you know I haven't signed that yet. So, the absence of the last signature renders the contract invalid. It was you who told me all of this. So now, I am changing my intention. I'm backing out. Out of everything. Why would I need revenge when Kerem is coming back to me? If I have to pay a compensation fee I will, I can give you all my money, everything I have, please, I'm begging you to cancel this deal."

"It's principles that are effective here, Miss Berrak; not begging. I couldn't be a malicious one if I ran my business at everyone's whims now, could I? Who would take me seriously then? On the other hand, I do have some sympathy towards you due to your father's passing, as I have stated before. Remember the form you filled out when you first came in here? My secretary had mentioned that you had to read the text in the form that was written in italic in case you changed your mind... Did you read it?"

"No, I didn't. It was written in such small font that it was almost meant to be overlooked."

"You shouldn't have overlooked it. You should have read it."

"What did it say?"

"We herewith declare that should a client back out of the agreement and refuse the services, they are obligated to carry out the following provisions:

Should the client back out of the agreement, they will be bound by the malignancy covenant for the rest of their life. This covenant is binding for fourteen years, or two Saturn years. The client is forbidden from ever thinking of, doing, or planning any malignancy about the matter for which they have come to Cabbar el Badisi. Should the client's frequency drop to 12-15 Hertz Beta level three times in these fourteen years; the plan for which they have come to Cabbar el Badisi will be automatically re-activated. Should the re-activation be triggered, it cannot be stopped even if the client states that they do not wish the plan to be activated.

"Can you be more clear on the meaning of this?"

"It means, if your vibration level falls to the aforementioned frequencies, I will be activating the third option which you have chosen in the beginning."

"Oh my God, that's terrible! How do I avoid that? I want to understand it completely, what exactly does that mean?"

"12-15 Hertz? I'll explain: three bad thoughts, three obsessions, three profanities, three small negative moves, and just like that, you fall right down to that frequency, Miss Berrak. So, if you want this love and this relationship, you must never let your frequency fall, or else, you'll be back here at my mercy. That's what was written in italic on the agreement. You would know if you had read it. It is almost impossible to keep your vibration levels from falling to that frequency. Especially with a difficult person such as Mr. Kerem. But you must remember, Miss Berrak: the minute your vibration levels fall, the agreement is re-activated. I wish you happiness under these conditions. See you soon."

"No, you won't."

"So, Miss Berrak, you are saying that you can keep your energy levels at high frequencies. You are saying that you will achieve the impossible. You are sure you can be so good for so long?"

I have to keep my frequencies high. How do I do this? What if Kerem doesn't answer his phone again, will I manage to not get angry then? What if he changes his mind about marrying me again, will I be able to keep myself from being depressed and continue to love him just the same? What if he upsets me, checks out other women when we are together, what if my frequency falls involuntarily? Then the plan is back in action. God, what kind of test, what kind of terrible torture is this? What if I feel like he's falling out of love, what if he leaves me again, what if he hurts me... So be it. If Kerem is coming back to me, then I am going to

141

live this love to its full extent: with the good and the bad, the hard and the easy, never giving up, not being possessive but giving him my unfaltering love. I don't have any other options. I cannot lower the frequency, I cannot get angry, jealous, petty; or else I lose him, I lose my life, I lose myself. Dear God, please help me, help me with this love and protect me from my own darkness. Point me in the right direction… Good God, please hear me… No, I am going to do this, I am going to experience this love to the end. I will make it, and no malicious one will be able to stop me.

"Yes, Mr. Cabbar, I can do it. I will do it for Kerem. I will do it for this love. I will do anything for this love. I will go above and beyond. I'm a Scorpio, remember?"

They say there are three Scorpios: lizard, snake, and eagle. The lizard, which is the crawler, was the Berrak who came here because she had been suffering, who wanted revenge, who begged Muhteşem to save her, who faced stooping seven levels below the floor as long as she got her revenge, who wanted Kerem to be just as devastated as she was. But that Berrak has died with this text message. The lizard has been crushed away.

Now, there is snake Berrak, a level above the lizard. The snake does not crawl, it heals, it won't hurt you as long as you let it be, watches you, integrates, sheds skin. Transforms. But still incomplete. It's in limbo in some way. I was in limbo when I received this text message.

As for the eagle type Scorpio: now that is a special one. Eagle is at the top level. It transforms itself entirely, carries a generous beauty within its heart, has an unlimited capacity of kindness, and it prevails against jealousy, darkness, and the desire to go under the ground. An eagle that flies up to the Divine levels of the sky. Now, that eagle is the highest level that a Scorpio can reach. That eagle emerges with victory from the eternal battle between ego and existence. Right here and right now, I am intending to become that eagle, and I am sealing this intention of my heart to infinite moment with this vow. I will prevail, I know it, I believe it. I will keep my frequency high. Your plans will never come to action, Cabbar el Badisi. I swear that I will succeed.

I will become an eagle for Kerem.

I will fly to eternity for this love…

To infinity…

21st of August, 2016, 02:12

İstanbul, Kadıköy

www.ingramcontent.com/pod-product-compliance
Lightning Source LLC
Chambersburg PA
CBHW030612130626
46552CB00002B/527